Stories of romance, society and madness

My deepest gratitude to David Sunderland, who proofread this book and to Andrea Luz Sanchez, who made its cover.

The Congolese dawn

Part One: Marcio El Pucho Aguirre
Chapter One: The interview

At a table in a small cafe in Paris sat Marcio Aguirre smoking a cigar. Even in the smoking capital of the world, a cigar was out of place: an anachronism and foreignism that did not fit France at all. But it was the first time Marcio had been to France, so he still needed to get used to its customs. Even in a multicultural city like Paris, this emblematic figure clashed with his surroundings. Even in one of the most progressive countries in the world, El Pucho Aguirre was a little out of place.

Of Spanish descent, Marcio had a pale complexion and undulating dark brown hair, which he wore long and uncombed; however, the natural curls helped keep his luscious hair tidy. Marcio had been born in a small village in Gran Buenos Aires and had moved to La Plata to study. He'd finished his studies in philosophy and had been disenchanted by the intellectual aloofness that characterized philosophy, which may have been the reason why he spoke in a prosaic and even rather crude way, in order to better convey his meaning. His family, back in Argentina, was composed of his father, mother and two sisters, who didn't speak any foreign languages and had no intention of leaving their country.

The reporter was fifteen minutes late, but Marcio didn't notice; it was ingrained in his habits not to care about time: "Just another capitalist invention," he'd say to anyone who asked. The reporter was a beautiful blond Parisian woman in her early thirties; it certainly seemed that her journal knew how to get to Latin American revolutionaries' hearts. Marcio had seen prettier women; he'd traveled all around Russia, Ukraine and other Slavic countries, but he knew from the moment that she started speaking, he'd be swirled into a state of fascination and fall in love immediately and irrevocably till the moment she stopped speaking. Because, for a Spanish speaker, who's used to communicating in a plain language with simple phonetics, listening to French is a treat for the ears. And there she was, unprepossessing, walking towards him with a resolute smile that seemed not to be out of politeness but out of a real adherence to his views. They had not only found a pretty girl for him, but they'd also found one who really admired him. "Salut," she said, in a casual manner that set the tone for the whole interview.

She asked him about his plans for the future, whether he thought of starting a family or writing, getting into politics or maybe just fleeing to a hidden place in Patagonia where he wouldn't be bothered by the media. He was enchanted by her questions, half because of her French manners and half because they were light and pleasant questions, not the usual ideologically serious inquiries he was used to. For a moment, he felt as if he was simply talking to a girl in a bar, just occupied with the romantic things people do when what they do is less important than who they are. But suddenly a couple of questions brought him back to his sad reality.

"Why did you go to the Congo in the first place? Why not any of the other countries in the world under oppression?"

"We don't choose our situations; our situations choose us. I knew that if I stopped to think about why I was doing this, why not something else, I'd end up doing nothing."

"So I'm happy for the whole world that you've acted so impulsively. You've actually hit the nail on the head; you've made the right choice, by mere chance maybe, by an extraordinary intuition more probably, but right after all."

"Aren't reporters supposed to ask the questions and the people interviewed to give the speeches?"

"Yes, sorry, that's off the record. I just got a little carried away."

"Don't worry, you can add a little of what you said to my answers, just to make them sound better, you know …"

"Thanks, but you're the hero, the person with real value; I'm just a nice speech in a nice dress, but you made the revolution possible."

"We're all nothing more than speeches; I just happen to be a speech with a gun."

"In any case, we're all happy that the weapon is in the right hands."

Marcio insisted on accompanying the reporter to her apartment, although she felt a little awkward because that would be totally unprofessional on her part. But she agreed in an ambiguous way that didn't show whether she was flattered, glad or simply too embarrassed to turn down his offer. Marcio was a man of action, not of thought, simply because he'd decided to be so. He was also a solitary man because his situation demanded it. But he didn't know if he wanted to be what he was anymore; now that the revolution was over, he'd need to resign himself to the fact that his life was meaningless at that time. People would always admire him; his fame was carved in marble. But he couldn't live off his fame; he needed to find a new purpose in his life. Maybe everything could start with an act of chivalry, even though it had been centuries since Cervantes had done away with the whole idea. So he walked her to her door and asked her if the phone she'd call him from was her personal phone and whether he could call her while he remained in Paris. She asked him how long he was staying, to which he simply answered, "As long as it takes."

Chapter Two: The beginnings

When Marcio was still studying philosophy at the University of Buenos Aires, he couldn't focus on Aristotle's, Sartre's and Kant's ideas; he watched the news and it talked to him about something else, something deeper than philosophy, something more transcendent than metaphysics. He believed in the elevation of the spirit by meditation on life's origins and final goals; he believed that life was just a span in our eternal existence, but he also believed in happiness and he didn't think it was compatible with injustice. From his early youth he'd been very moral, sometimes analyzing for hours, at bedtime, his daily actions. He was incapable of falling asleep whenever something he'd done fell short of his ethical values. From Aristotle he'd learned clear-cut ethical rules, from Sartre he'd understood that we're inherently free and that this is not so much our prerogative as our responsibility, and from Kant he learned to organize his thoughts. But he needed to balance this excess of Western-centered worldviews by reading authors like Tagore, from who he learned about our spiritual connection with the world.

The clash between the post-modern accelerated lifestyle and the contemplative nature of philosophy threatened to split his mind and spirit, especially when he needed to swallow great amounts of inane philosophy just to regurgitate it without analysis or assimilation. Fortunately, his faculty was quite progressive at that time, so they were able to have a more reflexive approach to learning. However, Marcio still needed to connect with the world in a more substantial way, so he watched documentaries about the world's misery, which seemed to be an endless subject. So, in a rash attempt to cover the sun with a finger, he focused on one single evil among all evils. In an act of self-delusion, he strove to believe that if he solved this single problem, there wouldn't be any more misery in the world. He was sure to be proven wrong, but that didn't detract from the fact that he found euphoria and even hope in this simple illusory act.

Marcio was a fervent fan of Che Guevara, not personally but ideologically. Che's Quixotic romanticism, his fearlessness and abnegation were an oil lamp which had consumed itself, but not without having left an indelible mark on the collective consciousness. Marcio wasn't an altruist and he had no intention of becoming a martyr; therefore, he subscribed only ideologically to Che's views. That was why Marcio was interested in the problem of the Congo, because it represented what Che had fought for: overturning the imperialistic system. He read up on all the issues related to the situation in that country, which might seem too intricate to people who aren't bold enough to take sides, but which looked very simple to him. The more he learned about it, the more he realized that everything came down to capitalism. Capitalism was a pernicious habit, a drug that ended up consuming the consumer. Marcio understood very well the capitalistic security fallacy, which he'd explain to everyone who cared to know about it.

He thought capital means security only in a world ruled by capitalism; otherwise, it is just what it is: an unnecessary waste of effort. The error lies in the assumption that capital is capable of regenerating itself ad infinitum, when we know from reality that nothing grows forever, that everything works in cycles. With capital, as with everything else, there's an initial period of growth followed by a period of consumption. The problem is that some people think that consumption and growth are compatible when they actually exclude each other. The international banking system promotes the illusion that there is a sort of productivity threshold, a capitalistic heaven where everyone can stop working and just live off capital's inertia. But capital, like everything else, needs care to grow, so what we're actually doing is replacing the production of utilities with the production of uselessness, that is to say capital.

The Congo was for Marcio just an outlet for his outraged emotions. His obsessive nature made him want to focus all his attention on one single purpose. Rather than bettering the world around him, which he found a trivial task, his patriarchal hunger for the attainment of goals led him to channel all his efforts into one cause: the economic liberation of the Congolese people. To do this, he needed to solve practical matters, like – for example – finding a way of communicating with them. This task would prove to be the most difficult one, but with perseverance he managed to meet Congolese activists who spoke English on the Internet. As is always the case, his revolution was meant to be a pacific one. He'd come from a safe background where he'd never been in a situation where he had to choose between killing or dying, so he hadn't planned on violence, but people are naturally reluctant to change, and whoever wants to bring about a big change is bound to find resistance on his way. Marcio had to make a great mental effort not to fall into passive acceptance of the current state of affairs in the world. He didn't believe in violence, but he believed in inaction less. He knew that some of his actions were bound to provoke violence as a response, but that was the opposition's choice, not his responsibility. Most of all he believed in the redemptive power of justice and he trusted himself as a judge of the world. Moreover, justice cannot be at the mercy of fear and peace is never attained but through real justice, so he arrogated to himself the task of improving the world, an arrogance that could've cost him his life.

Chapter Three: Like sheep to a shepherd

For Marcio, summoning up the willpower to leave his past behind wasn't a conscious effort but a mere concomitant of his resolve to go to the Congo. His was a fearless attitude born from uprootedness; he'd changed the comfort of a life of peace for the distress of a nerve-racking situation. After finishing his studies, he managed to get a turist visa to the Congo and a plain ticket visa to Kinshasa, not without first contacting everyone he knew there to ask for logistic aid for his revolutionary enterprise.
Once in the Congo, he didn't delay in getting out of Kinshasa to go in search of the revolutionary enclaves. To his surprise, the rebels were within reach of everyone who cared to find them; this was a challenge to his conviction that he knew about the situation in the country. He realized that, unlike Latin-American revolutionaries, African revolutionaries were more reckless and ostentatious. It seemed that some of them were rebels just for the higher status it conferred on them. There was an aura of resignation among them all; no one believed they could be redeemed, but some of them played the role of valiant soldiers just to spice up their lives. Many Congolese would've been happy if the white rulers simply stopped massacring people and destroying whole villages while they

exploited their land. None of the Congolese thought of the land as theirs; they didn't care about concepts of nation or territory; they only wanted the liberty to meander tranquilly through the vast Congolese plateaus and savannahs.

At first sight, it seemed pointless to stir up a revolution in a nation that had no cohesive fable or common culture; they didn't even have a single language but spoke different languages which sometimes weren't mutually intelligible. The main socio-political gap in their nation was the existence of two distinct ethnic groups, the Hutus and the Tutsi, who were irreconcilable. However, Marcio was well-known in his circle for his determination. He seemed to have taken upon himself the task of instructing his fellow revolutionaries. He gained the respect of his comrades by simple consistency. At the beginning, he'd been an oddity whom everyone listened to with wide open eyes, but after a while his words started to make sense to everyone and they adopted his words as an integral part of their ideology. Because the Congolese rebels were as brave as rebels can be, as fearless and selfless, but they lacked an ideological framework to give sense to their aimless rage. Marcio would impart his daily instructions to the group of Hutu rebels he'd joined and they'd listen to his every word as if magic could come out of his mouth at every moment. Marcio would say things like:

"We aren't communists; we are anti-imperialists. I don't want to be a martyr and that's my advantage. Rebels who're ready to die for their cause are alienated from society; they're seen as deranged people who haven't found pleasure in life and seek respite in death. I want to be happy as much as everyone else and I'm as selfish as every single person, which actually shows that everyone can change the world if they dedicate thirty percent of their energies to it, as we're doing. We're coming back home to our wives and children; we aren't giving our lives for an aimless cause. The group doesn't need cowards or deserters. We're meant to win the battle against wild

capitalism; whoever doesn't believe that the system is faulty and will collapse from its own weight can leave at any moment. We aren't terrorists; if someone commits a crime, he should be handed in to the authorities. We demand fair and reasonable things, but the emperors of this world will try to demonize us. So be ready to behave like saints and to be treated like criminals. But remember that we're just agents of the revolution and not revolutionaries; so anytime that you're feeling like protagonists, remember that a revolutionary's destiny is to live like a hero and die like a dog. So we won't be heroes, but we won't end up in a pit covered with mud and straw."
Everyone knew about Marcio's romantic oddity; it had slipped from his mouth once and it had been murmured among his followers since then. He'd fallen deeply in love with a girl who'd broken up with him because she didn't support his idea of leaving Argentina to go and get himself into trouble. From that time Marcio had let his hair grow almost untrimmed. He'd once said that his sorrow, the same as his hair, would never stop growing. Some people were deeply amused by this, but when they heard Marcio talk – or rather not talk – about it, they felt compassion for him. Whenever someone raised the topic, Marcio fell into silence or simply left, as a passive way of discouraging those kinds of questions. From the hints that could be gathered from his reactions, his followers knew he was brokenhearted and had put all of his mind into his revolutionary project. Despite their disagreement with Marcio's corny romanticism, people still respected his pain. After all, who were they to question the heart of such a conscientious man?
Some of his disciples, because after a few months of instruction that's what they seemed like, got into the habit of seeking advice from him about any possible sphere. One of them would seek him at meal times, when he knew that Marcio was more affable, and raise various issues, to which the following kind of conversation ensued:
"She says she isn't in love with me anymore. She says she's falling

for Thomas."

"Forget about petty affairs with women. Let your ideals be your only duty; life will sort itself out."

"But I miss her with every single part of my body."

"We never miss what we don't have; we miss only what belongs to us. Make sure you understand you've never had that girl and you'll be rid of memories."

Other times some rebels would hesitate about their cause or course of action, and conversations like the following one would develop:

"But Pucho, righteousness is on our side, so we must win, no matter how or when. Because either we're right and we fight with conviction or we're wrong and we'll be defeated by our own doubts and fears."

"So how can you be sure that we're right and they are wrong?"

"I just know it. Otherwise, what are we fighting for?"

"We're fighting for victory, remember that. And whenever we see a risk of defeat, we won't fight."

"Doesn't that make us cowards?"

"No, that makes us victors. Just remember this well: we don't fight hopeless battles."

"But we need to combat evil; we can't just stand by. We need to fight; we have the right to win."

"No one has the right to win. You need to learn not to underestimate people. You think you're the only sensitive person around? Everyone's dreamt of sweet love under Sunday sheets; everyone knows the difference between right and wrong, but what's right for you may be wrong for others."

"Do you mean to say we're fighting for nothing?"

"No, I mean to say we may die for nothing, but we're fighting for freedom."

"Freedom from what? If we're wrong, if this whole cause is meaningless, what evil are we combating?"

"Our personal evils. You're combating faithlessness; I'm combating boredom."

In the Congo, Marcio discovered that he was allergic to mosquito bites. He had to live for a few weeks with walnut-sized cysts on his body, to which were added crippling bouts of acute asthma, which had worsened due to the fact that they lived out in the open, with constant exposure to the humidity of the climate. However, that didn't interfere with his indoctrinating vocation, which went as far as teaching the art of war:

"You must know that every revolution, if not quickly effective, ends up being labeled as a terrorist campaign and its members end up persecuted and killed like criminals. Just take, for example, Che or nowadays, the FARC. Their only fault was a lengthy revolution, which earned them the antipathy of the people. If the people are an illiterate mass, let's educate them before starting the revolution. A country can't be governed without its people's consensus. Our current task is propagation; once we've gone to the limits of expansion, we'll start the summoning of forces, and just when we're ready, we'll attack swiftly and with all our might. If we succeed in dealing a blow that destabilizes them, they'll fall from their own weight. We won't attack the wounded beast of prey; we'll let it die from infection or bleed to death. We're not a subversive force; we aren't here to overturn the system but to make it work for our benefit. We're against capitalism, but not against their precious capital. By the end of this revolution, we'll make sure that every Congolese person has an account and some dollars in savings. We'll play by their rules and defeat them at their own game."

Chapter Four: The day after

On the day that followed his interview, Marcio knew that he'd found a new goal in his life. He came out of the lethargy he'd sunk into after the end of the revolution to find himself full of life again. He was a single-minded person so he took the same approach to all kinds of ventures. In his revolutionary enterprise, he'd been ideologically consistent, but conciliatory rather than aggressive. He'd sought a resolution to the problem and he'd avoided violent confrontation. He'd smoothly achieved his goal, without unnecessary friction. Now, in his approach to his new objective, he'd stick to his guns and summon up courage, because he was venturing into unknown territory.

He texted the reporter, whose name was Aurelie, that same day. He simply asked if she was free that afternoon and she answered, after a few hours, that unfortunately she had some reports to prepare and she'd be working till late. Marcio's experience as a military leader had been short-lived, but he'd had profuse experience as a bachelor, so he knew that love wars were more subtle and unpredictable than political wars. While political wars were decided by politics, economics and strategy, love wars were decided by mere chance. However, the maxim of war applied to both spheres: everyone loses in a war and it's paramount to avoid it. So the real martial art is about avoiding danger, taking what can be taken and giving up what's unnecessary to us. In close combat, a real warrior divests himself from encumbering armor and goes to the battle brandishing a single weapon, to show his enemy what he can expect. He seeks to disarm and not to kill and if he's disarmed, he surrenders and begs for mercy.

The next day she agreed to see him in between two interviews she had. They dined in a nice restaurant and she insisted on paying the bill. She was a liberal woman, but she wasn't a feminist. She was aware of gender inequalities in society, but she was also grateful to have been born in France, where she could develop herself in a way that wouldn't be possible in many other countries. She was concerned with social issues in the world and that was why she'd decided to make a career in journalism. She believed that ignorance was the source of all evil and she'd made it her life's purpose to bring wholesome information to everyone. Hers was a very moral job, because she needed to constantly purge herself from biases and fatuity, but she did it with responsibility and hopefulness.

She showed interest in Marcio, but he didn't know whether it was political or personal. She inquired about his personal life, but he didn't know whether she wanted to know him better or just to have a better picture of a revolutionary's background. He thought it was really disadvantageous to go out with a reporter, because he'd always feel interviewed, but he made a conscious to effort to give her the benefit of the doubt. He chose to believe she was just trying to gain intimacy with him and that gave him pleasure, so he didn't hesitate to leave aside his apprehensions and to participate whole-heartedly in his date. He didn't hold back with regards to romanticism either; he was romantic by nature and he showed her his affection so frankly that there was no place for doubt in his amorous demonstrations. He'd brought her a flower and he sought her body the whole evening like a moth seeks the brightness of a lamp in the darkness. His hand tried to clasp itself to her waist like a wandering thistle. His eyes roved around the ceiling, the floor and her hair just to catch her eyes unawares.

Everything was done in such a virulent tempo in order to be both overwhelming and exciting for her. But honesty demanded that he play out his excitement. Like a careless kid, he smeared her face and hair with his imaginary drawings. She wasn't particularly encouraging, but she didn't resist either. This neutrality on her part was a spur to exertion. At the end of their meeting, he felt both tired and fulfilled; he'd fed his need for possession and he was satisfied for the time being. He knew that the following day he'd have to exert himself again just to reach the same degree of closeness he was enjoying at that moment, but he left those fatalistic thoughts for later; now he was happy.

Chapter Five: The consolidation of forces

May the brothers be united
that's the fundamental law,
because if they fight each other
they'll be devoured by outsiders.
- José Hernandez

A crowd of three-thousand Hutus were standing in the valley when Marcio arrived with a megaphone. He stood ten meters away from the nearest man and started shouting in Hutu: "People from the Hutu clan, today is the first day of the rest of your lives! Your past is abolished from today! From now on, you'll be only what you decide to be!"

No one understood what he was talking about, so a funereal silence fell on the crowd. Marcio went on: "You've spilled your brother's blood and your families' blood has been spilled by your brothers; you've done wrong and it's time to stop this fratricide!" Some shouts of deep sorrow and rage were heard among the audience. "There comes a day when you need to decide between the perpetuation of evil and forgiveness. This is your Judgment Day! You'll be judged by the worst judge: yourselves! Those of you who've stained your hands with your brothers' blood, let your own conscience punish you! Those who have their hands clean, follow me in the building of the Congolese nation!"

The noise of the loud crowds continued, their yells and cries overlapping for twenty minutes. Marcio had a hard time shouting and straining his throat, trying to make them keep quiet so he could go on speaking. At last, relative silence was restored and he went on, "But for the building of a Congolese nation, the reconciliation of the estranged brothers is necessary. Today you will shake hands with your enemy and he'll stop being your enemy and become your brother again." The indignation among the crowd was so great that it started disbanding into groups, some of which walked away. The groups that remained were so loud and out of control that it was of no avail to try to shout over their voices. The people were so upset that they stopped paying attention to Marcio and started shouting things to each other and showing their indignation in various forms before getting the hell out of that place and abandoning this lunatic to his lot. However, some of the people saw what Marcio was doing at that moment and they elbowed their way to a place from where they could better see what he was actually doing. Some other people instinctively turned their eyes towards the place their neighbors were staring at and were hypnotized by the singularity of Marcio's actions. The general feeling was a mixture of astonishment and intrigue. They were already starting to think that Marcio had finally lost it and was completely out to lunch. They stared at him with deep concern; after all, they didn't wish him bad and they were sorry for him. Marcio stood in front of them with a pair of scissors in his hands. It was unlikely that he'd gotten them from someone in the crowd, so everyone assumed they were part of his plan. At his feet lay a mass of dark hair that looked more like freshly shorn wool. He finished cutting off his hair diligently and meticulously, which took him at least five long minutes. By then the crowd had fallen into silence again, so he raised the megaphone to his mouth and said, not shouting, but very clearly and with a hint of extreme anguish in his voice, "This is the first day of the rest of my life. From now on, I'll stop being my past and I'll join you, Congolese brothers, in your struggle for the present. Accept this symbolic sacrifice as a tribute to your courage."

That was all he said because emotion started strangling his voice. People knew that the sacrifice he'd just made was more than symbolic; it was real. And they also knew that his sacrifice had been made a while ago, in the confines of a small village in Argentina, where he was a happy man with a sweet girl in his arms. Although the Congolese were tough men, born and raised in one of the roughest places on earth, they still understood love and happiness, and they understood that Marcio was one of them by choice, which brought some of them to tears. Marcio was too excited to speak and they were afraid even of approaching him; a distance of ten meters was still kept in an act of respect towards this singular man, this alien that had come, like the Little Prince, to the most desolate confines of the earth, just to ask for someone to draw him a lamb. At the top of the hill, hidden by rocks and with the sun on their backs, stood three-thousand members of the Tutsi clan: The ones that had heard Marcio's call and had managed to come. There were two- hundred radios among them and all of them were tuned to the same frequency. They hadn't missed a word of what Marcio had said; he had put a transmitter in his backpack in order for them to hear. They couldn't understand the full meaning of Marcio's words because they hadn't seen his shorn head. However, they sensed the solemnity of the moment and they hushed each other to hear better. They were waiting for Marcio's voice of command and they heard it: "Now let's receive our fellow men, our kindred, blood of our blood, let us stay in peace while we wait for our Tutsi brothers to come." They started descending the hill, cautiously but firmly, towards their enemies.

When the Hutus saw the Tutsis coming there was a stir in the crowd. However, the stir was suppressed in its bosom because it couldn't burst out. If they wanted to attack the Tutsis, they would have to run over Marcio, who was in their way, and no one dared to do that. After half an hour of tense expectation, the whole Tutsi group seemed to finally be in their position, twenty meters away from the Hutu crowd. Marcio spoke, "I know that many of you still harbor rancor and revenge in your souls and I don't expect you to hide it here just to let it burst out in the middle of our revolutionary project. That's why I'm telling you this: If someone wants to kill a brother, let him step up here and fight me first. If you win, you'll have your revenge, but if I win, you'll humble yourselves and agree to be part of the greater cause." At first, no one understood what the challenge consisted of, so Marcio repeated, "I said that if you have murderous intents, come up here and play them out against me. I offer myself as the first recipient of your rage."

A few minutes were necessary for the crowd to grasp the full meaning of Marcio's words. They didn't want to fight him, but they didn't want to leave their enemies unpunished. The challenge seemed to them a good opportunity to have an advantage over their enemies by defeating their common leader. However, for most people, this was just a mad idea; they knew that as soon as Marcio was dead, the clans would engage in deadly combat. But their deep-rooted feelings were more powerful than reason, so people pushed their way to the head of the crowd with the intention to fight that arrogant man in front of them. People from both crowds formed bunches that waited just for Marcio's orders to show their bravery and fulfill their revenge.

Marcio said, "Let the first brother from the Hutu clan come and fight me."

All the rumors were hushed and some breaths were held while the most decided one of the Hutus made his way up to Marcio. At first, he just stared at him with all his pent-up anger, but then he charged him with all his might. Marcio step aside from the man's blind rage and barely avoided the butt of a forehead in his direction. The man was much heavier than Marcio and his arms and chest were twice as thick. Some people thought of intervening in Marcio's favor, but they didn't want to disobey his orders and do something that could endanger the momentary truce between the clans. Marcio managed to agilely slip away from the man's blows and charges, and he even attempted a few blows himself; however, the people were concerned about the result of the combat.

It happened suddenly, like a snake bite. Marcio leaped aside from the man's charge and dealt a quick kick to his ribs. The man fell to the ground shrunken like a sleeping dog. He remained there, giving no signs of standing up. Marcio went for his megaphone and shouted to the men, "Take this brother back home and let a Tutsi brother step up, if he wants to fight."

He started taking on the rest of fighters one-by-one in combat, first a Tutsi member, then a Hutu member again. The only rule was to fight barehanded, like a man. Some adversaries were a head taller than Marcio, but he managed to kick them in the ribs or in the pit of the stomach in a way that left them unable to fight for a good while. Another rule was that no one had two chances to fight, so once they surrendered, they had to promise to agree to his rules; it was just a question of honor, and no one would allow this agreement to be broken. However, after the fifth adversary, Marcio started to show signs of extreme fatigue; he barely managed to punch his opponent. The sixth man had a stout body that instinctively stuck to Marcio's in a suffocating embrace. Marcio couldn't escape this embrace and he didn't have a chance to deal his knockout blow; he was doomed. Marcio's opponent didn't let go of his grasp; like a boa constrictor, he just tightened his clasp on his victim in a slow but irredeemable path to death. Marcio gasped for air, his face red and his eyes bloodshot, until he fainted. The man let go of Marcio and stared at him on the floor like a kid who's just killed a bird. He didn't know what to do next; no one knew. The impasse lasted half-a-minute; they were all looking at Marcio, who seemed to be alive but utterly defeated. Suddenly, someone from the same clan as Marcio's opponent stepped into the fighting ring. He slapped the man on the face so hard that the man fell to the ground and remained there clutching his left ear with both hands. The man who'd stepped up shouted, "If anyone still wants to fight, let them fight with me! Otherwise, let Marcio's will be done!" Another minute went by, in which no one answered. A hand seemed to be raised somewhere in the Hutu crowd and a voice was heard saying, "I'll fight you, you son of a bitch!", but no one saw it clearly because it was immediately lowered by a neighboring hand, whose owner said, "Shut up, you bastard!"

Marcio then stood to his feet slowly but steadily and then suddenly shouted, "Now let the brothers unite in a common embrace!" and he went and grabbed a Hutu member by the hand and brought him to the middle, where he stood until Marcio brought a member from the Tutsi clan. He took both of them by their hands and make them shake hands. Then he went on bringing people from both clans to the middle until, like children who have learned the drill, they started doing it by themselves.
Thus peace was made between the Hutus and Tutsis.

Part Two: The story telling

Chapter One: The empanadas

Marcio was exhilarated by his meeting with Aurelie the previous day. He'd read her one of his horror stories and she'd shown her appreciation of his creativity and descriptive abilities. He'd inclined himself towards storytelling and writing during his long campaign in the Congo; he hadn't wanted his mind to become numbed by social interaction and physical activity, so he wrote some short stories that by chance had a tinge of horror in them: "The main attribute of a short story is its surprise effect," he said, "and the uncanny is the most powerful surprise element." He admired Edgar Alan Poe, but he had also read an Argentinian short story writer, Horacio Quiroga, whose examples he followed. In the solitude in which he'd found himself, dedicating himself fully to a social cause and not being able to take care of his personal life, he'd resorted to writing to find some intimacy. He was sure that lasting friendship is not struck up where political interests are at stake and, unfortunately, his social and economic revolution was also a political one. That is why he wrote some horror stories, which he shared with whoever liked literature. Some days, a group of twenty to fifty people would encircle him while he told one of his freshly baked stories. His were tales of real horror. No ghosts, no walking dead people were involved; they were just stories about the infinite human capacity for evil and madness. His first story was born one day when his group was asking him about his life back in Argentina. He knew they meant well and that they thought their questions were flattering to him, but they didn't know that Marcio was immune to compliments and that it was already the umpteenth time that he'd repeated himself. So he decided to play a joke on them and he invented a story whose surprising effect was increased by the fact that everyone thought he was relating a real event. Later on, they would ask him to retell this story, which had fascinated them, and which they called: The empanadas.

I was walking one afternoon, as usual, to kill time until my wife came back home to dinner. She worked full-time so I was in charge of the household. I didn't mind the cleaning because it was a small house. I loved cooking and I didn't mind washing the dishes, so that wasn't a problem either, and my wife helped with the washing and ironing of the clothes. However, I felt uncomfortable taking care of my child. He was a blond one-year-old angel with one eye blue and the other brown. I liked watching him play with his mother and smile at her, while he uttered some indecipherable sounds and clasped his little hands to her clothes and hand. However, whenever I held him in my arms, his eyes lost all their brightness and his smile faded. I even fancied that his eyes turned brown before me and became blue only in his mother's presence, but whenever I told this to my wife, she just broke into laughter.

The afternoon was calmer than usual. The empanadas were ready, waiting in the oven till my wife came back; I had cooked them on low heat so they wouldn't lose their juiciness. For those who don't know, empanadas are a salty pastry filled with various ingredients. That day I had chosen my favorite filling: red meat. I always seasoned it very well, so the different flavors would blend with an indiscernible pleasure on the palate. It would take at least half an hour till my wife came back and I didn't like hanging around with food in the oven, because I was always tempted to open it and tax the dish with a mouthful that I took out of mere impatience and gluttony. So there I was, passing by the butcher's and reading the promotions: 10 zl for a kilo of boneless pork seemed an offer no one would let pass by, but that day I didn't feel inclined to consumerism. Besides, my wife didn't like meat as much as I did, but I hoped that would change after that day's meal. I'd always been afraid of vegetarianism sneaking into our home.

I had walked for a while and I was passing by a park full of pigeons. I was a fervent carnivore and I had always thought that wherever there are pigeons, people can't die of hunger. Sometimes I imagined shooting at them with a sling and bringing one or two back home, just to see if they tasted like chicken. But some people disabused me of this idea by telling me that urban pigeons carried many diseases. Thus, I gave up my hunting fantasies just to dedicate myself completely to domestic activities such as changing diapers and making sure the kid didn't cry while my wife was sleeping. Of course, we took turns at these tasks, which was more than fair to me, but I still couldn't get used to this ultimate act of civilization: caregiving. I always supposed that taking care of a child of mine would be a mere instinctive act that would kick in as soon as I saw my progeny in front of me, but it hadn't happened as expected. The more I tried, the more awkward I felt in front of that child; it seemed that he could guess that I was making a fool of myself and he enjoyed humiliating me. The mischievous fiend would start crying as soon as I put a hand on him and finish only when I'd finished changing his diaper or cleaning him up. My wife had grown weary for this reason and she blamed it all on my carelessness and lack of attention. She'd showed me a hundred times how to hold the kid so he wouldn't cry or how to play with him so he'd laugh, but my movements and gestures were just a pantomime of what they should've been, so in the end she'd taken upon herself all the tasks that were related to the child and I did all the cooking and cleaning to compensate. I was more than happy with the deal and I could at last enjoy the pleasure of watching from afar, with admiration and fearful respect, that small dictator becoming a human being.

I was lost in my thoughts when suddenly my mobile phone rang. It was my wife; she was coming back from work and she was calling to find out how everything was going. "Everything's in order." I said "The food is ready already. I got anxious and cooked it a little earlier." I turned towards the house at that moment and quickened up my pace because I had been wandering aimlessly and I was quite far from home. "Where are you?" She asked, "It seems like you're outside the house." "No, I'm just on the balcony," I said, so as not to upset her. For some reason, I knew she'd be upset if she knew I was outside. "So I'm getting there in five minutes sharp," she said, "and I'm hungrier than a wolf; I haven't had breakfast this morning." "I hope my dinner won't disappoint you then," I said, but I wasn't sure that it wasn't going to be the case. She always talked about the advantages of vegetarianism and the savagery of carnivorism, but she still ate meat out of consideration for me.

I walked faster and faster till I found myself running back home; I hadn't noticed that I'd walked in the same direction for twenty minutes and now I needed to get back in just five minutes. There were no tram lines that could help and it was no use putting myself at the mercy of a bus and its mysterious schedule. Therefore, I just ran and, to my surprise, I got home one minute before my wife. That gave me time to turn off the oven and display the empanadas as if in a floral arrangement.

When she got back home she went straight to the kitchen. She just took her coat and boots off, but she was still wearing her scarf and beanie when she took the first bite from her empanada. "Mmmm," she only muttered and "mmm" again; all her senses were evidently enthralled by the empanada. But as soon as she'd finished her first one, which was just three minutes after she'd taken it, and that was only because the steam coming out of it had prevented her from eating it faster, she got up and headed toward the bedrooms. I grabbed her almost violently by the arm; I couldn't believe that she'd eat only one empanada and then leave, without showing any sign of wanting more. She stared at me and, as she understood my hurt feelings, she smiled at my naivety. She told me, "Please don't eat them all; I'm just going to check on Johnny." "Johnny," I thought, "who could be so mean as to give such a name to someone." But one second sufficed me to realize that that was my son's name; I just hadn't gotten used to it yet. "He's OK," I said. "Don't worry; he won't cry anymore. Just eat another empanada." And she stared at me and I knew that at moment she'd become vegetarian.

Chapter Two: Bedtime story

One night, when they were sitting around the bonfire, the talk was centered around women. For this group of men, accustomed to everyday harshness and months of exile, the absence of female company was something that didn't demoralize them. However, whenever they had a chance, they'd boast about their feats with the women in their villages and they'd philosophize on the character of those paradoxical creatures. Marcio listened to them merrily. He'd had his share of experience too and he related to them in most of what they said. But he liked keeping his intimacy to himself, so when they asked him about his experiences with women, he said he wouldn't speak about his experiences in particular, but he would give them a picture of what Argentinean women were like in general by telling them a story that may have happened or not, but that accurately described the character of Argentinean women. Thus he started telling them his Bedtime Story:

Emi was preparing to go to sleep, although she wasn't sleepy. At her grandparents', bedtime was at 10 pm, which was a huge contrast to her bedtime back at home, around midnight. She'd always bring along a book so she could stay up reading until sleep arrived. However, this time she'd forgotten to bring one and the ones on her grandpa's shelves weren't interesting to her. Her grandpa was an amiable man and she loved playing chess with him, helping him around in the garden and sitting on his lap listening to his fantastic stories. He was a great storyteller and her imaginary world grew exponentially with every tale she heard from him.

But that day her grandpa had a cold and he'd gone to sleep already, so asking him to tell her a bedtime story was out of the question; she'd have to resort to her grandmother. Now, that was by no means a good option because her grandma, although she cooked like a chef and was very generous when it came to presents, was by no means a storyteller. Her grandma would readily read her any book she had brought, but she was unable to create a single storyline or to give birth to imaginary characters in a consistent fashion. Whenever she attempted to tell her a bedtime story, she would get lost in the plot and get all the characters jumbled up; her original characters tended to disappear as the story progressed, as if swallowed by the earth, and new characters tended to be created out of thin air, so in the end the story of a princess that wanted to go to the moon ended up being the story of a sailor that proved that the Earth was round. Even for a six year old, these gaps of coherence were so evident and the whole story was so dissonant and illogical that she couldn't sleep afterwards due to thinking about what had happened to the pretty princess or what Columbus had to do with the whole business.

But Emi had a generous heart and there was nothing else to do at her grandparents' because, in old people's fashion, they didn't have computers, and the TV was off after 9pm. So she decided to give her grandma another chance so she could redeem her disreputable storytelling skills. Therefore, when her grandma kissed her goodnight, she said:

"Grandma, could you tell me a bedtime story?"

Her grandma looked disoriented as if she'd been asked to put out a fire or assemble a car. However, after fifteen seconds of hesitation, she said:

"Just one story comes to my mind right now, but I don't think it's suitable for a child of your age."

"A child of my age!" – Emi was upset at this blatant lack of respect for her mental maturity – "Grandpa retold me Anna Karenina and I understood it all, so I think there's nothing I can't take. I'm an adult," she affirmed, full of conviction. Her grandma couldn't find arguments to dissuade her granddaughter so, after mentally cursing her husband, she started telling her story:

"Once there was a man."

"What was his name?" asked Emi, worried that her grandma would start mixing it all up again.

"Mmmm, his name," – her grandma thought for a while – "his name was Carlos."

"Like grandpa!" exclaimed Emi enthusiastically, and she laughed inwardly at the thought that her grandma had said that name

probably just because it was easy to remember.
"Yes, so Carlos was a young man visiting some old friends back in his hometown. Although he was originally from Junín, he had recently married a pretty girl and they lived together in a small flat in downtown Palermo. His friends, a married couple, were thirty years older than him; they had been very good friends with his parents and, after his parents had died, they'd become his only link to his hometown. They were very fond of him, so whenever he went to his hometown, he was sure to have a place to sleep at their house."

They had a fifteen-year-old daughter, called Beti, who had almost grown into a woman at that time. Beti was very shy, but her shyness betrayed hidden passion rather than fear of people. She was a tall slim girl, her eyes were the color of honey and no one that saw her would deny that God existed and had modeled her with His own hands. Carlos was an affectionate man and he kissed and hugged his friends, but he couldn't get close to Beti, so he had to wave her good morning when he arrived at the house, to which she answered with the same gesture. During the morning and afternoon of that day, which was a Saturday, Carlos chatted with his friends to catch up with them, he ate their delicious food and read a book he'd brought with him. Beti was always around, now listening to music, now reading a book, now watching TV. She seemed to be totally indifferent to the fact that there was a guest. "The new generation," thought Carlos, and he hoped that his own children would behave less autistically. For a moment, he thought of his young wife back home and he was sorry they hadn't had a child yet.

In the evening, his friend invited him to drink a bottle of whiskey that he'd reserved for a good occasion. Carlos was a little lightheaded so he got drunk much earlier than his drinking companion. The drinking soiree was over at 2 am because his friend was dozing off on the sofa while they talked. The house was quiet and dark because the ladies had gone to sleep hours ago, so Carlos groped his way into his room. He didn't want to turn on the light for fear of it burning his bloodshot eyes. However, he could see the silhouette of his bed thanks to the moonlight entering through the window. Just when he'd lain down fully-clothed on his bed, he realized a warm body was beside his. He turned his head thunderstruck; it was Beti underneath the covers. For a moment, he thought he'd entered the wrong room and he felt utterly ashamed, but then he saw his belongings on the table, where he'd left them that same morning. He thought that maybe she didn't know he'd be sleeping there, so he stood up to leave the room and go and sleep in the living room, when he heard her whisper, "Please don't go." He remained paralyzed by pure fear for twenty seconds. All his blood had rushed to his temples and he was scared at what he might do if he stayed. "I need to go; I can't stay here," he said, and he felt a pang of guilt at what he had just said, because it implied he wanted to stay. She had known that he wouldn't leave the room; she had known it from the moment he'd laid his eyes on her that morning. She sat on the bed, showing her pale nakedness, and she undressed him delicately but firmly, first his T-shirt before moving to his pants and ending up with his socks. He didn't stir, as if fending off his guilt by convincing himself that he hadn't done anything wrong; he was just too drunk and that girl would eventually realize that what she was doing wasn't appropriate and she would stop. But she didn't. After undressing him, she took her panties off and got into the bed with him. The last thing he remembered was her warm body pressing against his before he lost all control of himself.

The next morning, when he woke up, she wasn't there anymore. It took him an hour to summon up the courage to get up, and another hour to subjugate the fear that overcame him every time he tried to go to the kitchen and stare at his friends' faces. However, after exchanging good mornings, everything became easier. They treated him in the same way as they had treated him the day before and that convinced him that life would go on in the usual manner, and that the previous night had been just an extraordinary exception. "New day, new life," he said out loud, and his hosts laughed cheerfully, not understanding the whole meaning of the phrase. For the rest of the day, he didn't see Beti anywhere. That fact scared him slightly, but it also relieved him. He had the strange idea that if nothing came to light that day, it would all be buried and forgotten for ever. In the afternoon, as planned, he bade goodbye to his friends and drove back home. He couldn't stop thinking of Beti during the whole journey; he was worried his wife would one day learn what had happened, but no, it wasn't that which worried him the most. He was scared of himself; he couldn't recognize himself in the actions of the previous night. "It wasn't me," he thought. An idea started to permeate his mind: "Maybe it was all a dream, a very vivid dream. After all, I have a strong imagination and I was very drunk. Definitively that wasn't me last night; I'd never behave in that way except in dreams." This idea soothed his conscience and by the time he arrived home, he was just glad to see his wife again.

She was making dinner and she had run out of pepper, which she added to every meal, so she asked him to go to the shop nearby. He was happy to comply with her demands, but he couldn't seem to find his keys. "Just take mine," she said and gave him a kiss with her thin lips. Suddenly he remembered a passionate kiss from a red fleshy mouth, and he cursed his mind for playing tricks on him. He descended the stairs and more images came to him, as if the fog that had covered them were gradually clearing. He took the pepper from a shelf in the shop, while two thin but muscular legs entwined themselves around his waist. He paid at the checkout while two thin but strong arms pulled him towards them. He ascended the stairs to his flat while waves of long hair cascaded on his face. When he got to the kitchen, he was exhausted. He couldn't repress his feelings any longer; he must tell her, no matter what; otherwise he'd drive himself crazy. She wasn't there, so he went to the bedroom. He saw her wearing a different dress, her back towards him. But a second sufficed him to realize that it wasn't her; it wasn't her hair, her hips or her legs, it was ... her.

Beti turned around and told him, "Don't worry about your wife. She won't be between us anymore."

He didn't have the strength to ask for details and everything was just a nightmare, so he did what everyone does in a nightmare: he ran away. He searched in the other room; it was empty; then in the bathroom, and there she was, his wife, laying in the bathtub, covered in blood.

"I think I'm pregnant with your child. I can feel it," the girl said behind his back. "Nine months later your mom was born," said the grandmother, concluding the story.

Emi hadn't blinked during the whole story. "But ... your name isn't Beti," she said. "You're Grandma Elena." And she stared incredulously at her grandma while she saw her go out of the room. After a few minutes, she came back with a piece of old paper. It was like a little notebook, which she handed to Emi.

"This is my old ID," she said simply. "After the story I told you about, I had to change my name. Of course, no one should know about it; I hope you'll keep the secret for me."

"Of course, Grandma," said Emi, glad that she was given a secret to keep. "So goodnight, Grandma ... E-l-e-n-a," she said, making it clear that she'd never pronounce her real name, while handing back the piece of evidence.

"Good night, darling," her grandma said, and she kissed her cheeks. "Now that's a good story!" said Emi to herself while she was getting into her bed, and through the whole night she slept like an angel.

Chapter Three: The walled door

The group had loved his horror story because they hadn't expected it. The next time they asked him for a horror story, they were expecting something horrific to happen, so Marcio decided to be subtler in his delivery of horror. He told them the following story:

Jack was a simple man, but he was also a writer. He couldn't help expressing himself on paper; it was in his very nature. The whiteness of a blank sheet was an open invitation to him to draw from the deepest corners of his heart some phrase or vivid image that could touch other people. In other spheres of life he'd achieved a significant level of functionality that allowed him to be considered a non-handicapped person. But it was true that he had to put twice as much effort into doing things that for other people were as simple as breathing. Instead of rejoicing when he found a good job or passed an exam, he just felt that life was void of meaning and all his actions were senseless. Also, instead of seeking closeness in interactions with the opposite sex, he just sought animalistically the warmth of another body and the ephemeral possession of its superficial attributes. At the most intimate moment, his eyes had the glassiness of a surgeon's and the avidity of an artist's. There was no love in them; they didn't look to see but to possess, to exploit the body in front of him. However, he didn't do it by instinct or to fill the void of a faithless life, as many people do; his life was led by aesthetics and he had an aesthetic purpose in everything he did. So at the most intimate moment, he sought beauty instead of love; he opened his eyes and tried to catch a glimpse of beauty instead of closing them and letting himself be replenished by the cosmic soul that breathes into the communion of two bodies.

But that was the doom of a writer: to be able to describe love, to see it happen, without being able to embrace it. He could write thousands of books which would stir the soul of everyone who's ever felt that cosmic love, but he could not feel it himself. To be a surgeon in whose hands lies life itself, who could destroy it all by a simple twist of his wrist, but who's unable to possess the secret of life itself, that's the sad privilege of a writer. Oh blessed are those who've loved without thinking, those who believe without seeing, because only their hearts can be touched by happiness! But those who've eaten from the forbidden apple, those who've dared go beyond the limits of propriety and have seen what the eye is not prepared to see, those have no salvation!

Thus Jack had felt from the moment he'd stopped being a child and had taken his first deliberate step towards beauty. He'd read books he didn't need to, some of which had awakened a primeval characteristic of his soul. He was too conscious to live among people, so he'd had to resort to numbing substances just to be able to function in a world where reality and fiction were clearly distinguished. He'd written it all down; he'd put it all into a book, all the miseries of his soul. More than a book, it was a chasm into which he'd thrown every single thought that was not proper enough to be uttered.

He'd recently finished the book, which he'd called The Walled Door, and he'd sent it to his publisher. He'd already published a couple of books, and he had a small public and some sort of a literary reputation. When he'd handed the manuscript to his editor, who always insisted on having them on paper, he'd seen the sparkle in his eyes and heard him say, "The Walled Door! I'm really intrigued." Around the same time, he'd met a beautiful and lovable girl called Dagmara. She'd caught his attention as many girls had done before, but she'd increasingly endeared herself to him and now he had no intention of leaving her. It was with the utmost distress that he'd told her about his new book; he was extremely ashamed of it and he would've burnt it for her sake were she to insinuate that it could endanger their relationship. But she was very lighthearted and she

soothed his apprehensions. She asked him what the most terrible thing he'd done was and after he'd racked his brain to try to choose from among a plethora of options, he confessed his worst sin and was immediately absolved. After that his heart was light too; he felt nothing she could read would scare her away from him. He knew her to be valiant and not faint of heart; he felt he could trust her to have the courage to weather the dark storms of his innermost self.
But he still didn't know if he could trust himself. Although he grew to love Dagmara, his appetite for new experiences didn't wane. His book became a bestseller and people praised his honest style. And it was all true; his writing was nothing less than honest. He'd described events in his life in detail and his most intimate thoughts and emotions lay naked on the pages of his book. Fortunately, the critics and readers had not known how to decipher his messy plots and they could never guess which parts of his novels corresponded to his real life and which didn't. But he knew, and he also knew that he was becoming more predictable. His plots didn't fascinate him anymore; his writing came to a standstill. Dagmara noticed it and tried to laugh this problem away at first; then she tried to convince him to take a break from writing and take a job as a university professor that had been offered to him. This he refused bluntly; he was a good writer and he'd proven it; by no means he was going to quit his vocation. She didn't complain; she tried to help rediscover his inspiration and they both lived on the royalties of his book, which were starting to dwindle, and on the income from her job. She was as happy as usual, but Jack felt miserable due to his lack of inspiration; he started analyzing himself to try to find the cause. He concluded that he was too happy to be inspired; he'd been lulled into comfort and there was no drama that could trigger a new novel. He'd tried looking for new subjects, but none was appealing enough to him. The only subject that matter to him was love and he'd drop every other subject as soon as he started writing about it. But he had

no new ideas in the romantic sphere; he was happy and there wasn't anything else to say. Of course, there were domestic problems, and many nuances which he could've described, but he wasn't interested in these petty affairs; he was interested only in epic love.

She could bear anything; he wasn't mistaken about that, but there was one single thing she couldn't bear: his unhappiness. At first, she tried to cheer him up; then she tried to arouse some emotion in him with her tears and at last she resorted to shouting and provoking him. She made use of all her feminine artifices, but she wasn't able to recover his enthusiasm. He started to seek solitude again and she allowed him. Then, when they met, she'd be all joy and kindness; those moments with him would become more precious to her as they were becoming rarer. But it happened one day that Jack told her simply that he wasn't in love with her anymore and that it would be better for them to break up. She accepted it without a tear; she'd gone the distance and now it wasn't the moment to cry but to put on a brave face and summon up courage for the next phase of her life. However, she asked him a favor, more for himself than for her. She asked him to start a new novel but in an unconventional way. She told him that his novels always revolved around the same topic: a love story. He knew it, so he agreed with her and listened attentively to her advice. She told him he must rewrite the ending of his latest novel, The Walled Door, and that that should be the beginning of his new novel. That was simply brilliant, and he couldn't wait to start implementing her advice. She asked him to give her a last kiss before she left. He kissed her, but it was a passionless kiss, which didn't stir any emotion in him. However, when she left, that kiss was the trigger for an idea for his new novel. It all started with a kiss, a kiss the main characters of his latest novel had given each other almost at the end. Now this kiss, instead of being passionate and full of hope, was deprived of feelings. Now the female character of his love story, feeling the coldness in her lover's lips, had despaired and had thrown herself from a bridge and had been enveloped in the coldness of the waters of the river. Now his main character was single again and his heart, although mourning the loss of a lover, was still susceptible to love's sways.

He went on writing for two days. His new book had a sad introduction that set the mood for the whole story; however, he was thinking that love would help heal his character's heart and would eventually redeem him. He was ready to introduce the female character; he just couldn't find a name for her. It was late so he decided to drop it till the next day and he went to sleep. The next morning he was woken up by the police. They'd found Dagmara's corpse; it had been washed ashore. He couldn't believe it; he asked how and when it had happened. They told him that probably he was the last person who saw her, because she hadn't spoken to anyone else for the last two days; besides, they thought that was the minimum time needed for a drowned body to resurface. They felt his statement that they'd broken up that night supported their idea that it was suicide.

He was desolated. He didn't know what to think. She'd seemed so calm that night; she hadn't even cried. And what was really strange was that he'd written it! For God's sake, he'd predicted it! He read what he'd written, just to check whether he hadn't gone mad; the paragraph was there, with the words written by him: "Then she jumped into that flowing river as if she were jumping into the flow of eternal life." Then he remembered something that chilled him to the core: it had all been her idea. She'd asked him to change the happy ending of his latest novel. That kiss was the turning point; that single kiss had started this whole nightmare. He ran to his bookshelves and found the copy of The Walled Door; he wanted to read those lines again, those lines of a past in which he was happy and he could think about his life with enthusiasm and passion. He wanted to remember through his book that past that now seemed so far away.

He leafed through the pages until he found the scene. The characters were there, the same place and time but ... "Oh, the horror! All the horror of a perfidious world, all of it here and now!" Where before there had been a passionate kiss, now there was the coldness of a loveless character and the despair of a woman who walked silently but determinedly to the bridge. Now she jumped "into that flowing river as if she were jumping into the flow of eternal life." And at that moment Jack stopped making the extra effort he'd always unconsciously made for his heart not to stop beating and he died, putting at last an end to the single love story that had run through all his novels.

Chapter Four: Blank pages

Now the men just wanted horror stories. After all, what other feeling than fear can grip you so much in such a short period? Marcio had no problem creating horror, which he believed to be inherent to people's minds. The only problem with horror is when it's alienated it from our psyches, when it's externalized by creating fantastic creatures or events. So Marcio tried to keep it simple:

The alarm went off at 8 am, but Pablo got up at 9. That morning, as with many others, he had a strange feeling of monotony. Blank pages lay on the living room table, together with the pen he'd spent half-an-hour looking for the previous night. He walked to the toilet, where he washed his eyes with cold water and he went to the kitchen to make himself breakfast. It was a Friday, but it could just as well have been any day of the week, because all days were equal to him in terms of activities.

He watched some news: Argentina had thrown in the towel and had made a more than appealing offer to the vulture funds to come out of technical default and a woman had been attacked by a polar bear in northern Russia. The doorbell rang; his American friend had arrived. He had come to the city for a few days and had asked Pablo if he could stay over. He opened the door and greeted his friend, but then went straight back to writing his short story. He wanted to finish it, but he didn't know why; it was probably just the thrill of writing that was more powerful than any other feeling he had at the moment. But he was also thrilled that day because of a date he was having in the evening. She was a beautiful girl he'd met a week before, and she was the only reason he was going out that day. He still had eight hours until his meeting with her, eight full hours that he could dedicate to his short story.

His friend was an amiable guy, but a little too talkative in Pablo's view. However, this time he didn't seem to have much to say; he just sat at the living room table with his laptop and after asking for the Wi-Fi password, immersed himself in his computer. Pablo was glad and he continued handwriting phrases on the blank sheets of paper. He belonged to the dying caste of writers who still handwrite their first drafts because of the sensual pleasure they feel when they move their hands over the white sheet of paper, smearing it with ink as if they were smearing a lover with their creational seeds. The living-room light was a little dim so he brought a lamp from the bedroom. "What to write about?" was Pablo's only concern, "Maybe some basic stuff, like the description of someone's everyday activity to start with, just to make it evolve into an unexpected delirium. What about eating something first? He asked his friend if he was hungry and he made lunch. After they'd eaten, his friend went back to his computer and he continued with his writing. "Should I write a romantic story? Maybe something based on my expectations of my imminent date." But it was so trivial; just a date with a girl that might become his wife or not; nothing else to say about it. So he decided to focus on his professional fears, of which he had many, like – for instance – how to earn a living from his literary writing and where to draw constant inspiration from. At the moment, he had *odd jobs that drained the writing spirit out of him; basically he felt he was wasting his life on worldly matters, like financial security and girls, and that he'd regret it someday. Because in his spirit there was an eternal fight between his propensity for happiness and his need for writing. He didn't know what he wrote for. He wanted to be read and recognized by many people, but at the moment of writing he didn't care whether his works were going to be read or not; he just felt the urge to fill the existential void of an empty sheet of paper.*

So he was going to write a romantic story after all; that was the only topic at hand. He could fantasize about the potentialities of his date; she might end up killing herself for him or giving him some blond kids who would spill miscellaneous liquids on his papers. Yes, that was a great subject, so he started developing it. He based his character on her: not on the girl he knew but on the girl he imagined she was. In his story she was beautiful, as well as in life, and smart and talkative, just as much as in reality, but in his story she was also deeply melancholic, although he'd seen no sign of it in the real her. In the story, she became increasingly disabused of the fantasy that she could ever be happy with him; she became easily irritated and desperate in the end. In his story, she abandoned him and the blond progeny that had populated his living room went off with her. Now his character found himself alone in the solitude of his house. How to close this story? He looked at his friend, who was still on his computer. At that moment, his phone sounded. A message from her: She excused herself because she wouldn't be able to come to their meeting. He proposed some other day, but she simply told him she'd let him know when she was free. At that moment, his friend got up and told him he was staying at someone else's place that night, but he'd come back the next day if it was OK with him. Pablo told him he could come by whenever he wished and stay over when he needed to. When his friend left, Pablo racked his brains for a suitable ending for his story, but he couldn't come up with one; it was late and he was mentally exhausted. He regretted it all: the canceled date and the sad story he'd written; in a destructive impulse he got the pages he'd written and, taking a lighter, he set the papers on fire in the sink. Then he watched a romantic film he'd already seen, and then another, until at last he got sleepy. He laid some new blank sheets of paper on the table, but couldn't seem to find his pen. He looked for it for half-an-hour; it was in the bathroom for some unknown reason, but he knew he was absentminded so it didn't surprise him. He just laid the pen on the table and went to sleep. When he had almost fallen asleep, his phone sounded again. It was her, but the message was strange. It said: "I don't know what happened to me today; I just freaked out for no apparent reason. We can meet tomorrow at the same time, same place if you want." Pablo agreed to their meeting as he had no plans for Saturday. Then he set the alarm for 8 am, as usual, and went to sleep, planning to write a new short story the following day, as usual.

Chapter Five: Political commitment

Aurelie's reactions to Marcio's horror stories weren't what he'd expected. She was a woman inclined to politics and her artistic streak wasn't very developed. This unveiled a facet of Marcio's character: his political one. He found himself arguing with her about issues in Europe and the world. The thing that reassured him whenever he disagreed with her on a subject was that she respected Che Guevara and thought his ideology was good, although his implementation of it had been wrong; the same as with Marx's ideas. They both agreed that Guevara and Marx had been the symptoms of a soulless capitalism, and that they had known how to identify its problems, but hadn't known how to deal with them. With that stronghold secured, he could argue with her about anything, even the nonexistence of God, totally undeterred by the outcome.

It was a time of political unrest in Eastern Europe, and Marcio was living in Europe at that moment. Everything he heard in the news sounded biased against Russia to him and pro-American. But fortunately there was democracy in the mass means of communication, and this democracy was called the internet. There he found some insightful ideas, some pragmatic and others more idealistic. He particularly liked an article that was written in an amateurish way, probably by some passionate idealist, but which struck him as a very honest peace of writing. The article was called:

On the U.S. plan to militarize Eastern Europe

"For all who draw the sword will die by the sword." - Matthew 26:52

Please Latvia, Lithuania, Estonia, Poland, Bulgaria, Romania and Hungary, don't bring the temperamental watchdog to your property. The United States is a snappish Rottweiler that may give you a feeling of safety, but only if you understand safety as bombing your house every time a burglar breaks in. I may actually be insulting Rottweilers by comparing them with the U.S.; after all, Rottweilers are at least loyal. But the point is: Do you really want to deter violence by bringing violence into your bosom? And if you don't believe American foreign policy is violent, where have you been in recent years? Have you forgotten the Cold War? Have you forgotten Vietnam? Are you aware that the States is still at war against communism and pursuing a quest for global domination? Do you believe the States is doing you a favor or that it is just using your dear territory as a potential battleground? But, most importantly, do you believe the Americans are the good guys?

I understand your apprehension towards the militarized Russians and I'd like to live without fear of invasion too, if I were from a country so near to Putin's unpredictable Russia, but haven't we already seen how the U.S. deals with conflicts? Do you want to

*exchange the fear of invasion for the certainty of an escalation of
tension that will end with a war on your territory?*

*Just to give you some key information before you make your
decision, in 1997 NATO and therefore the States had actually
promised Russia not to bring "additional permanent stationing of
substantial ground combat forces" near the Russian border, a
promise that the U.S. is blatantly ignoring, as it does with moral and
ethical issues in general. An unethical peace is just a justification for
rebellion. In the management of a society, like for instance the
global society, there are always conflicts of interest; if we don't
allow for them and we believe that consensus can be imposed by
force, we'll just make space for legitimate violent rebellion, as is the
case with terrorism right now. We all agree terrorism is horrific and
inhuman, but we all know they have good reasons to react as they
do: despair being something you can't argue against.*

*I'm not against the police; we all need a system of deterrents to
control ourselves, our actions and speech. But we try to sharpen our
moral sensitiveness in order to act as best we can in a given
situation. What I mean by this is: do we really want the States to be
the moral standard of the world? Or do we believe that the police
can be amoral and they can be used just in the case of an
emergency? If we believe the latter, we're wrong. The police are
extremely moral; actually they place more importance on their
moral values than on their subjective esthetic and ethical views in
any given situation. That means that the police act according to set
rules; they do not create their own morals. If we know this, and we
know also the kind of moral principles the States' foreign policy is
currently acting upon, aren't we just wishing for the worst by putting
them in charge of global peace?*

*The States is childish in its approach to conflicts. It plays the game
of provocation: "I'm not attacking you; I'm just cocking my gun and
standing in front of you, watching your every move to detect a false*

step and shoot first, because that's always been my philosophy; just look at Hiroshima if you don't believe in my potential for mindless reactions."
A job interview with the States would sound like this:
"Mr United States, do you feel qualified for the job of police of the world?"
"Well, you couldn't find anyone more suitable for this position, if I'm allowed to say so, because, for instance, I dropped two nuclear bombs on civilian targets before realizing this battling method is not efficient in the long term; I mean, if we want life on Earth to survive a little longer than a couple of months of a nuclear war. So now I'm banning the production of nuclear weaponry in other countries and enforcing this law by shelling the hell out of them, of course. How else could I be respected after I've hit first? So that accounts for Iraq and it may justify North Korea in the near future. You know, my problem is that capitalism is my religion and, in that sense, I'm more fanatic than Spain used to be, if you know what I mean. But all in all, I think I'm qualified for this job. Who else would shoot a kid down today and come to work without any remorse tomorrow?"
Are we sure we want to give Russia a reason to despise Europe? Do we want to allow the States to bully other countries and to militarize every corner of the world? Do we believe guns are the best deterrent against violence? Do we want the world to improve or do we want to give way to fear and allow it to get rooted in our global society? Why are we still demonizing Russia? Hasn't savage capitalism taken more lives than the Russian invasions? Isn't a quiet Machiavellian system of global exploitation more destabilizing than Putin's open demonstrations of force? Is our society so desensitized that we don't see the roots of violence? Or do we really believe that an army can be more harmful than hedge fund managers without scruples, heartless corporations and belligerent politicians? I know there's no easy answer to this complex question, but I'm sure of one

*thing: I would never entrust the States with the protection of my
children.*

Aurelie had strong anti-American feelings too, which soothed
Marcio's scorched heart. She laughed at the article, which she found
interesting, but not very accurate. She had her own ideas on the
subject already formed and she was Leo by birth, so she wasn't prone
to budge from her convictions. A heated argument ensued between
the contestants and, in the end, Marcio conceded the match,
although, he thought inside himself, the game is never over. He just
didn't care about being right or wrong anymore; he just cared about
drawing smiles and expressions of surprise from that dear face in
front of him. He could've written the most trivial love song at that
moment, and its lyrics would include the trite verses:
*May the world lie in ruins and the stupidity of men work itself out,
may people for ever hate what they don't know, but
may a beam of sun caress your face, my love
so your smile will never wane.*

Chapter Six: The published author

When Aurelie heard one of Marcio's spooky stories, she
recommended he should publish them. She had some contacts in the
publishing world and with his fame, his stories were sure to become
popular. Everyone wanted to know about the deepest fears of such a
brave man like him. Marcio was flattered, but told Aurelie that she'd
change her mind about his bravery once she read his stories. Those
were very intimate stories for him, and he wasn't sure he wanted to
share them with the whole world. Back then, in the heat of the
revolution, they needed some distraction and the stories he told
provided it. No one analyzed what he said; they just liked it or they
didn't. But in a world of peace, the written word takes on more

relevance and people may start an argument and even fall out because of an unfortunate phrase or a badly articulated idea. He didn't want to be exposed to that kind of psychological butchery in which people conjecture about the reasons behind his writing. She told him that she believed people would appreciate his writing and they would not overanalyze it. They admired him already, so everything he did was going to be tinged by his fame. All those ambiguous things he wrote or the dark passages in his stories would be seen in the best light possible and people would read only the highest feelings in them, because they knew the man who'd written them couldn't be pusillanimous; so she implored him to have his works published. He bowed to her petition, not because he agreed with her about his bravery, but because he knew that, in this new phase of his life, the kind of courage he needed was totally different from the kind he'd needed in the Congo. There were no external revolutions to stir anymore, so the most fearsome battle was now going to take place: the internal one. He needed to define himself and take an ethical and aesthetic stand on life now that he wasn't busy anymore. He needed to decide whether he upheld tradition or liberalism when it came to love matters. He was falling for the sensual blondness in front of him; it was an animalistic magnetic feeling, but it had repercussions for his mind and spirit. He wanted to be fair with her and with himself; he wanted real love and he wanted to love her as well as possible. But what was love other than doing good to others? He didn't have another definition of this overused concept. For him, love was time and dedication; love was trying in earnest to make someone happy. But how could he love her? What did she need to be happy? Did she need him? And what if she didn't actually need him? That was the key question: was he indispensable to her? And how could he become indispensable to her? And, most importantly: was it fair for him to try it? Was he going to be able to provide for her happiness once her life was so entangled with his that a separation would be destructive for her? All of these questions were then summarized in one: Am I able to make her happy? Then his resolve kicked in.

"I'll send you a new story tomorrow or the day after," he said, "but it won't be a horror story; it'll be lighter."

"Well, I'm glad to hear it." she said. "Take your time please; there's no hurry. I'll send them to a few publishers as soon as your stories are ready."

Thus Marcio decided to start by gaining her admiration and letting himself be trimmed by her love. His was the flame of life, but hers was the lamp that was able to contain it. He wanted to be tamed by her and to become more civilized, more worldly and more sensitive to the needs of others. He drew nearer to her like the first wolf must have drawn nearer a bonfire, with fear but excitement. He caressed her back and then grabbed her by the waist. He pulled her towards him and pressed her cheek against his, hiding his mouth in his hair as if it were a beast of prey in the grasses of the Savannah. Then he slipped his mouth towards hers, like a stalking tiger, and pounced on her lips with a clasp that promised not to let go of them until she surrendered. And so she did. And they parted.

Now Marcio had both the inspiration and the reason to write a short story. He thought for a moment that, were everyone in the world to be asked to write a story, many would do it. He thought it was natural in people to want to share their thoughts and writing them down was one of the easiest ways to do so. He felt privileged for having the possibility to have his writing read by people and to be paid for it. It was a pleasure for him to write, so he wanted to write well to give some of the same pleasure to his readers. He thought that horror was one of the most selfish literary genres, because it is just an outlet for the writer's fears. He valued humor much more, because to make his audience laugh, a writer needs to know about the world and about other people's problems. To make people laugh, a writer needs to see outside of himself; he needs to be able to find the incongruous beauty lying hidden in everyday life. But Marcio was a brave man, and he'd try to achieve his goal. Thus, he wrote his first short story:

Weaning Charlie

Little Charlie was his parents' pride and joy. He was an adorable son, loving and playful, and he'd given many happy moments to his Polish parents. However, there was a flaw in his behavior that was starting to worry them: Charlie wouldn't give up suckling on a feeding bottle. Charlie was their first son, so they didn't have any experience in the matter, and they'd thought that this anomaly would eventually disappear by itself, but little did they know about Charlie's determination when it came to sucking on a feeding bottle. He spent at least an hour a day with the bottle in his mouth and, no matter what they did, he didn't seem willing to ever exchange it for a glass.

At first, his parents, who upheld the ageless Polish customs and traditions, tried to wean him on vodka and steak tartare, but this ended up being counterproductive. Charlie showed a little reluctance when they explained to him that a cow had been slaughtered and put directly in front of him to be eaten. He thought of the paradox that he was encouraged to wash himself every day and take care of his hygiene, because in that way, his parents said, he'd live longer and be healthier. But now the cow, who had been washed and kept in a hygienic state, had ended up being chopped and put into a small dish in front of him, ready to be eaten. He then thought that, were humans to develop a taste for raw Little Charlies, he preferred to be non-hygienic so people would think twice before having a bite of his tender flesh while he walked in the street. Thus, from that day, he refused to be washed and, whenever he could, he'd wallow in mud in the same way pigs do, so he was at least sure that he wouldn't be eaten by Muslims and Jews. The vodka, however, he didn't refuse, so little Charlie could be seen from that day on tumbling around the house whenever he wasn't sucking from his feeding bottle. Eventually, his parents managed to convince their son that a cow could yield ten times more flesh than him, so his flesh wasn't urgently needed, and that, in a civilized country like Poland, no one would be so impolite as to bite him in the street without his permission. Also, they hid all the bottles of vodka from him and whenever he asked for one they told him that it was politically incorrect to drink vodka now that Russia had invaded Crimea, which he understood perfectly.

One day Little Charlie met Berta, the neighbors' daughter. His parents then took him every afternoon to meet her; they were hopeful her presence would help wean him, but this proved to be even more counterproductive. Berta wasn't the kind of girl that liked to compete with a feeding bottle and when she heard of it, she was shocked. She told Charlie that it was repugnant for someone of his age to go on sucking from a feeding bottle. She tried to induce him to stop doing it by tempting him with other equivalent activities. She explained to him that his sucking habit had been already explained by Freud and that it was identified as oral anxiety; therefore, he could easily make up for the bottle with other things. Charlie was already thinking of the innumerous possibilities when Berta stuck her finger in his mouth. Charlie instinctively started sucking on it and went on for minutes; he found it so delightful, and Berta would've probably lost her finger had she not exchanged it for other parts of her body. However, Little Charlie didn't seem to give up on the bottle; whenever he was with Berta, he was OK, but when she wasn't around, he'd actually suck on his bottle even more than before. It seemed that Berta had actually exacerbated his oral anxiety instead soothing it. His parents didn't want to go into details when Charlie told them about Berta's ingenius idea; they just looked at each other with total resignation: now Charlie was addicted to the bottle and to Berta. They went and told everything to Berta's parents: Charlie's problem and Berta's unconventional treatment, and Berta's parents were shocked when they heard that Charlie still sucked on a feeding bottle. From that day on, Charlie would go to Berta's by himself because Charlie's parents were too ashamed of themselves for not having been able to wean Charlie from his childish habit. From that day on, they swore not to tell anyone else about it.

As the months passed by, Little Charlie seemed to be stuck in his ways and his parents spent sleepless nights trying to find a solution to their little darling's problem. They struggled with their worries for a long time until they decided to try something that, although it didn't change anything, might help to control Charlie's milk intake. Up to now, Charlie's bottle had been blue and it wasn't possible to see its contents. So they decided to buy Charlie a transparent bottle, which he liked from the moment he saw it. To his parents' puzzlement, Charlie's bottle was always filled with a transparent liquid. Up to that day, they hadn't controlled what Charlie filled his bottle with, but the fact that the liquid was transparent intrigued them. Their first thought was it was vodka, but, as traditional Polish people, they thought it inconceivable that someone could drink vodka in another way than by downing shots, so they dismissed this idea as plainly ridiculous. Then they thought it might be apple vinegar, which is known to be good for stomachaches and other ailments, but they didn't have that much vinegar in the house and they doubted that Little Charlie had bought it by himself. Then they came up with the easiest choice, which was so simple that they couldn't believe it was true: Charlie had been filling his bottle with water! Yes, simple tap water, directly from their kitchen sink! They grabbed at their hair in deep agitation and cried with relief. During all this time they'd thought Charlie was suckling milk from his bottle; the thought hadn't even crossed their minds that there could be anything else in a feeding bottle than milk, but there had been, and they couldn't keep their tears from flowing. But when their crying had got rid of the stress caused by their main worry, they continued to be puzzled. Why was Charlie drinking so much water? And why didn't he drink it from a glass, like everyone else? After deliberating about the approach they were going to take towards this new problem, they called Charlie.

Charlie was surprised to hear that his parents had thought that he'd been drinking so much milk during all that time. "Come on!" he said, "Did you really believe I'm able to drink five liters of milk per day? I'm not a calf you know!" His parents laughed their embarrassment off. They didn't know what to say; they'd deceived themselves into believing that their son had been suckling milk, when he actually was sucking water. "But anyway," they said, "Why are you drinking water from a feeding bottle and not from a glass?!" Charlie stared at them with an incredulous look. "Well, you go and try to drink five liters of water a day yourselves and then blame me for trying to find the easiest way! Do you believe I'd be able to drink five liters were it not for the feeding bottle? Then you're crazy." "So you mean to say," uttered his father, after a thirty second period of information processing, "that the only purpose of the feeding bottle is to help you drink more water?" "Am I correct here?" he asked, with understandable puzzlement. "Well, yeah!" answered Charlie, "It's been proven that we can drink more by using a straw or by sucking than by simply gulping liquids from a glass. I personally prefer sucking because straws are for girls."
His parents' stupefaction was so great that they needed to take a break just to pinch each other and check whether they were dreaming. Charlie waited till they came back to their senses and then he told them, in an offended tone, "I didn't know you folks

found it weird that I drank from a feeding bottle. You should've said something!" "But, but ..." mumbled his father, "But Charlie! Why in hell five liters a day?!" Again Charlie stared at them as if they were Martians that had just landed in his living room and taken the shape of his parents. "Why folks, don't you know that five liters of water per day is recommended for a good health?" "Wha-wha-what?" was the only legible sound coming from his mother's mouth; his father had fallen into a state of mental paralysis due to his brain's inability to process what he was hearing. In IT terms, his brain had just crashed. "Well, yeah, five liters a day! No more or less, I've read it online." "Whe-whe-where?" was the sound achieved with strenuous effort by his mother. "Well, on this blog about natural ways of living, folks! Come on, don't be so backward! It makes you feel lighter and more energetic; you should try it." "I-I-I'll-I'll try it someday, Charlie," said his mother, shoving his father into consciousness. "But are you sure five liters a day is not harmful?" "It's proven," said Charlie, "and many people do it." "Well, Charlie!" said his father in an authoritative tone, now seeing clearly through the mirage. "Many people jump from a bridge without floating devices, but that doesn't make it right, does it?" Charlie thought this over for a couple of minutes, his parents staring at him with worry, but also with infinite patience on their faces. At last he said, "I may have overlooked the fact that this method was created in California, where it may be hotter than here in Poland, so probably reducing the dose to 3 liters a day would do no harm." "I'm happy you've come to your senses, Son," said his father, grabbing him by the shoulders with the gesture of a father who's just recovered a lost son. "And I guess," he went on, "you won't need to drink it from a feeding bottle anymore if it's only three liters or let's say two-and-a-half per day. Because, Son, look, the most worrisome thing here is that you're sucking from a feeding bottle, and you're already twenty years old." "You're right! I hadn't thought of it like

Part Three: The war on capitalism

Chapter One

It was high time to do something. The liberation activists that had been sent to enlist people into the revolutionary movement had come back with documents full of names and data. These were people who'd agreed to take part in every form of revolution and who actually needed to have explained to them that there wasn't any current need of them to form a military force, but they were only asked to spread the news that a revolution was taking place. However, the activists expressed their sincere concern that if a revolution didn't start soon, these people would grow weary and would join an armed force. Marcio saw the problem and called everyone into an assembly. He'd finally set the aims and procedure of the revolution. Once everyone was quietly expecting to hear the words that would come out of his mouth, he addressed them.
"What's the aim of every war?" he asked. Many answered, but he rejected all the answers until someone said: "Defeat."
"Yes," he said. "A side wants to show the other side its superiority. This may be achieved by means of battles, in which a side shows its military superiority, but the disadvantage of this tactic is that some battles may be lost and the final score is not quite clear. What's then the ultimate factor that defines a war?" This time no one answered.
"It's morale. The victors are those who manage to kept their morale high enough to go on fighting. The defeated give up in the end, even if they've won most of the battles. In our war there'll be only one battle: the moral one. Once we've won that battle, there won't be any

need for further actions."

Everyone was confused by Marcio's words. Although they'd always been told that the revolution would be pacific, they still hoped for some form of military action. If not with the aim of killing the enemy, at least with the aim of establishing authority for the movement. They were disappointed by Marcio's words; they'd been recruiting people vehemently and they saw all their efforts betrayed by a lukewarm leader that didn't understand the urgency of the situation. Because everything was urgent in the Congo; nothing was done as a precautionary measure. People reacted whenever they saw a chance and they were a very brave nation that didn't fear death. They currently possessed the human capital to start an armed rebellion that would be difficult to quench and they were sorry they were going to miss out on this chance. Marcio understood them well and gave them some minutes to assimilate his plan. He killed time by drinking some water and talking to one of the activists about trivial matters although everyone thought he was actually discussing the issue in question. At last he addressed them again.

"What's capital?" he asked. Everyone was taken aback by this sudden change of topic. They had bargained for a socio-political rebellion and now they were receiving a lecture in economics.

"Money" was the first answer, which came out of mere frustration. "Not quite," he said. "Money is just a form of transaction; a way in which goods are exchanged and there's nothing wrong with it. It's just more convenient to carry money in your pocket than the products you've created and it's much better that your employer or client pays you with money than with products. But capital is different; it's wealth that's used to create more wealth. Capital is actually the opposite of money, because money is current while capital is hoarded so as to have an advantage in any negotiation. Capitalism plays the scarcity game. The idea is to monopolize the market by buying all the natural resources and the basic services, then to raise the price of these basic things so people are forced to work full-time. Because one of the most recent creations of capitalism is full-time jobs. People can posses the basic things they need to live for a fraction of the effort they needed two- hundred years ago, but capitalism finds a way to keep people fully employed. Here's where money comes in. Until now it was a simple means of transaction, but now, thanks to capitalism, it has also become a commodity. And because the law of supply and demand dictates that something that's scarce has a greater value, hoarding money makes the value of money increase. For this purpose, capitalism has created the perfect institution: the bank, whose main function is to hoard money. Now, money must be current; it must give the impression of flowing constantly; otherwise, it loses legitimacy. That is was why more money is constantly created by the banks, either by a deal with the government of by means of interest. Now interest is the key to the capitalist system; without it capitalism would cease to exist. Interest is an illusory way of creating money, because it assumes that money can produce more money. Of course, when more money is created, the whole value of money is reduced and inflation takes place: goods cost more or money is less valuable. But as money is created by the institutions that monopolize money, they only reap the benefits and they don't lose in the exchange; on the contrary, it's the easiest way to buy new things and keep the illusion of money as currency. But inflation affects everyone possessing money, because everyone loses purchasing power; therefore, everyone with a fixed salary is harmed and they need to resort to strikes or demonstrations to demand a general rise in salaries. But meanwhile they're robbed of their money because they're earning relatively less than before. All this money goes to the banks; it's the banks' taxation on society. That's how we inadvertently support the institutions that are subjugating us economically.

The good news is that every country creates their own financial system and their own currency, so no one is obliged to accept the global rules of capitalism. The second piece of good news is that the Congo is the poorest country in the world, if we consider human development, so we can allow ourselves to start anew economically; we don't have much foreign interest to lose. What I propose as the start of our revolution is a cold war against the Congolese banking system. Let's spread the news, banks must go down for the Congo to rise! We'll create national banks that will be for the service of the nation."

"How can we do that?" someone asked.

"In a democratic country like ours, there's no great inconvenience. We'll stop using the current capitalist currency and create a new one."

"And how can that make any difference?" another person asked. "Won't this currency become in turn a new capitalist tool of oppression?"

"No," Marcio said. "Because our currency will be backed by gold. We'll abolish fiat money in our country." Everyone was dumbfounded. Talking of gold to these people was like talking of champagne to a thirsty person. It was just incongruous with their actual needs. A whisper started spreading among them, but Marcio didn't alter his countenance; he stared at them with the iciness of a sculptor contemplating what to do with the piece of wood in front of him. When the whisper grew louder he raised his voice and said: "We already possess enough gold to feed our people for a decade, and that's all we need. If we establish a fair economic system where the currency actually flows, we don't need to worry about the global market or other nonsense of globalization. If we want to start dealing with foreign countries again, we need to have the upper hand. Now, we won't accept dollars as payment for exports but only our currency, which they can buy at the moment of the transaction. All the dollars that are thus acquired will be used to buy more gold that will enrich our state and make our currency still stronger. Of course, the state will provide a financial system that will allow for the acquisition of houses and other necessary goods at a zero-interest rate. We will restrain imports until the economy is stable and we'll never enter the global market again without the supervision of the state. Exports will therefore also suffer, but we already don't count on them for the sustenance of our people. We count only on ourselves. The only way to have healthy relations with foreign countries is through self-sufficiency. Now we don't have the political power to make these changes, but we possess the power of the masses. This is an ideological revolution and it will be spread by word of mouth, by pamphlets and any other possible means. We'll seek the authorization of the government, but we won't depend on it. This revolution is pacific, but we'll stand up against repression." Everyone saw the picture by now, although not everyone was happy with the exchange of a simple armed revolution for a convoluted economic boycott. However, they expected that as soon as the government got wind of the subversive aims of the movement, it would try to dismantle it by force. However, they weren't counting on the fact that Marcio's first action when he'd created the movement was to reach out to the official power of the country and establish means of communication with them. He constantly reassured them of the innocuousness of the movement and he was extremely careful to allow for a possible assault on him or some paramilitary means of persuasion against the continuance of the movement. However, he knew the government had greater threats and they didn't have the power to start an immediate military process to eradicate a movement whose leader was hidden somewhere in the Congo.

Chapter Two
The place where the revolution found greatest resistance was obviously Kinshasa. This city had been the focus of the expansion of

capitalism and the gate through which the Congo's wealth flowed abroad. There were many foreign interests in this city and they started making phone calls to their respective sources of political muscle. But they couldn't do more than put pressure on the president to uproot the budding threat to the economic stability of the country. People were massively buying gold and, when the price of gold in the country rose, they started exchanging their Congolese francs for the liberationist currency: The Congolese dawn. The liberationist movement took charge of exchanging the Congolese francs for dollars and of buying gold abroad. The government was making so much money on taxation that they turned a blind eye to it. They didn't see it coming because the vigor of the revolution was so great that it took only a month to deplete the streets of Congolese francs. Sellers started to accept Congolese dawns, although at half the value of Congolese francs. However, this didn't discourage people, who were proud of building a new country and saw the new currency as their dearest child. When the government realized the situation, it started printing new money, which actually devalued the price of the franc, which in a month was equal to the dawn. The government then declared the dawn illegal and burnt all the bills that entered its possession, but they didn't dare to arrest their users because the currency had become widespread. The people took precautions to prevent this measure from upsetting the movement: as every bill was numbered, every merchant that accepted a bill needed only to write down its serial number and it was promised they would receive one hundred percent of the value of the bill in gold at the moment of its loss. The merchants were happy to exchange a fluctuating currency for gold so they followed the plan. The government wasn't smart enough to put the illegal money they'd confiscated back into circulation, that is, to rob money from the people. They didn't do it because that would've been counterproductive to their aim: to wipe out the new currency from the Congolese streets. Instead, they hoarded the confiscated money, which provoked a great appreciation of the dawn. The government was now rich, provided they put the money back into circulation. Marcio and the government reached an agreement: the government would legalize the dawn, whose minting was going to be controlled only by the liberationist movement. The movement promised not to print bills to devalue the currency, but the government had to use the money they'd confiscated for the public good. The government then declared how many dawns it possessed, information which was roughly backed by the data base of declared confiscated bills. A development plan was also demanded from the government, and all the money was quickly allocated to the different projects that were going to take place in the following two years. The money was therefore sent to the Liberationist Bank to safeguard it. Then the Liberationist Bank and the government agreed on taking a measure to assure the stability of the currency. Evidently, with the inflow of all the confiscated bills, the dawn would be devalued, and that would result in a loss to the government too, meaning all those projects wouldn't come to fruition. So the Bank, before doing anything else, bought gold with the appreciated dawns it possessed, until it replaced all the gold lost during the confiscation. This move, once the Bank had declared how much gold it had in its vaults, appreciated the value of the currency even more. During the following two years of public works, the dawn lost a little of its value until it stabilized again.

With the financial problem solved, the Congo was able to take the reins of its own economy, to better manage its natural resources and even to expropriate companies that were bleeding the country. Its political muscle grew and, as it had enough wealth, it wasn't concerned with foreign investment or international credit. The Congo had set a precedent: distrust in fiat money, so it didn't take any credit. The Liberationist Bank grew in financial power until it could finance the welfare of all its citizens. Later on it financed the welfare of neighboring countries. The influence of the IMF on the world decreased, especially since the People's Bank of China followed suit and started lending money for welfare at an almost zero-interest rate. Other banks adopted this new trend until the IMF, the most resilient of all banks, ended up lowering its interest rates to continue having some dignified status in the global market.

Chapter Three: The Congolese War

Marcio was by no means a good military leader, but he was the soul of the movement that now was being persecuted by the government's armed forces. The Congolese movement had earned the enmity of Wall Street, which considered it a form of neo-communism. Therefore, it didn't take long for unofficial capital from the U.S to arrive in the Congo in order to crack down on economic subversion. With this new injection of American cash, the Congolese president became an adamant opponent of the revolution and he declared war on it. Marcio didn't have the required skills to win any military battle, but he knew that wars were won morally rather than physically. He divided the revolutionary forces into numerous guerrilla groups and risked his life crossing the Congolese borders. He went to Europe, where he talked to the media and, eventually, with members of the European Union. He knew that righteousness was on his side, so now the most difficult task was to make the Europeans interested in something other than themselves. He knew the Congo wouldn't hit the news until thousands of people were killed in the repression planned by the Congolese government, so he needed to try to depict the right image in people's minds by means of his words. He told them the story of his escape from the Congo. Had he been caught alive, he would've surely been made disappear, along with all his group, because there were no witnesses who knew of his location. They had been lucky. On their way, they'd encountered two patrols, one of which saw them and killed five members of their group. Marcio himself had killed a man, and he dwelt on it as a philosopher would dwell on any crisis in his life, and when people listened to such an intelligent man talk about the inevitability of his murderous actions, they feared for their own future. His detailed description of the situation in the Congo and the aims of his revolution were easy to grasp and adhere to. Many people felt like him in Europe and he knew it; he put all his hopes in European democratic power because he knew it had already achieved some selfless aims. After a month of campaigning and some thousands of casualties back in the Congo, the European Union agreed to a deployment of military forces throughout the Congo to allow for the Congolese revolution to take place peacefully. The Congolese president withdrew his forces from the streets and, especially, from the forest, and the American tycoons withdrew their money. The current president lost the next elections, and the new president was more sensitive to the needs of the people and the social importance of the revolution that had taken place.

Chapter Four: The sin of being rich

Aurelie wasn't the only person who admired Marcio, although she was one of the few people who knew him intimately. Since the revolution had taken place, Marcio had become a political figure and he'd been invited to give speeches everywhere: on TV, at political assemblies or simply at home, where his words would be transcribed and then published on paper. He was careful where he went, and he particularly liked giving speeches at universities and at gatherings at other places connected with education, as long as they were free of political bias. One of his most popular speeches was the one he gave at Harvard University, in the core of capitalism. Che Guevara and the Pope had previously ranted against wild capitalism and now, with a third anti-capitalist Argentinean figure, the world labeled Argentina as a nest of communists, in a jesting or aggressive way. But Marcio wasn't giving a speech for those who believed he was a communist; he was talking to those who, like him, saw many flaws in the capitalist system. That's why he addressed those American students as people capable of seeing and understanding the evils of the system they were part of:

"I'm thankful for this invitation to share some of my observations on this economic system we have. My speech today will verge on the religious because I think that the only way to change such a strong default system is by faith in something better. Now when we talk of capitalism, we talk of the belief in the materialism of the world, we talk of people who believe that everything can be bought. That's capitalism. If you just work to get enough money to afford a house to live in, food for your family and the possibility to learn and develop intellectually and spiritually, then you're not a capitalist but a simple human being. The problem with capitalism is that it just takes a few assholes to ruin the wonderful system we have: liberalism. This is because those greedy pigs don't believe in anything and they try to break other people so as to feel better about themselves. If we take a look at the reasons why most people commit crimes or deliberately harm other people, it's because they lack the essential means of subsistence. Despair is what pushes so many people into crime and violence. And this unnatural situation is created by the few faithless bastards that populate this world. These people really believe that the only way of improving the precarious situation of most of the people in the world is by promoting the pursuit of selfish interests. These are the people who think that the most important things are material and that the rest can be acquired at any time. These people don't put any value on solidarity. Now this is the evil of our liberal society and we need to get rid of it if we want it to thrive. The expropriation of private wealth would make no sense without an economic policy, because new rich people would emerge. A new economic framework needs to be implemented.

To start with, we need to revise our concept of exploitation and wealth production. Natural resources should belong to everyone and their exploitation should enrich every single citizen in a given country. Some international organizations already intervene to guarantee the sustainability of the world, and this is positive. But every country needs to guarantee its own ecological sustainability; otherwise, we're creating third world countries again: countries that are left relatively undeveloped, and which provide food and oxygen to the others, who thus continue exploiting them. Globalization is natural, whether we like it or not. The fumes exhaled by American factories provoke tsunamis in Japan and floods in South America; therefore, a global policy is needed. Being rich in this globalized world is a sin, because the wealth we amass and hoard is food that we're taking out of someone's mouth. We can't deny globalization and we can't close our eyes to the fact that there are strong links between the endemic poverty of underdeveloped countries and the supremacy of developed ones.

Chapter Five: Marcio's diary

Marcio lived happily with Aurelie till he died twenty-five years later from a heart attack. Of course, "happiness" is a subjective construct, but if by it we mean satisfaction with life and continual activity and development, then yes, Marcio was happy. When Aurelie woke up one morning and found him, at the young age of fifty-three, placidly sleeping a sleep from which he'd never wake up again, she cried from loneliness but also from happiness. She was happy she'd met him and made him happy throughout his whole life. She felt accomplished more than ever before. They'd had one son, who by now was already finishing university and was almost ready for complete self-reliance.

Aurelie opened Marcio's drawers for the first time in her life. From the moment when they'd moved into that house, there had been a desk, which Marcio had claimed for himself and whose drawers were opened only by him. There she found a diary from the time when Marcio lived in the Congo. There were some miscellaneous phrases; nothing worthy of being called "writing" or "ideas". They were simply "thoughts" from a mind probably derailed by the extremity of the situation it was going through. The notes didn't follow any pattern or order; they were written sidewards or upwards; probably depending on how Marcio had felt like grabbing the notepad every time. She read them meticulously, but also without interest. She already knew everything there was to know about Marcio and it was a closed case. She'd loved him and now she couldn't love him anymore, which anguished her because she needed to find a new outlet for this urge in her. She read through the notes, rather thinking of how to employ all this excess of care and time which she'd been left by Marcio's death. She was buying time by reading his diary, but she knew it wouldn't last long. Besides, reading can't really be considered an act of love but of selfishness. However, she went along with the task in hand; the current page in front of her read:

Don't idealize attraction. We fall in love with someone's looks, and there's no other way. The dichotomy: body and spirit to which many people adhere is false. Our bodies are the reflection of our spirits. Beauty is there to be admired, in men and women; there's nothing wrong in that. But we differ in our aesthetic tastes and that accounts for our not desiring the same type of people.

Titillating TV shows and movies, arousing selfish dreams and exacerbating the spiritual isolation of materialism. For once I wanted to make this about something else than romance. I wanted

this not to be another romantic exposition.
She closed the diary; her mind was made up. She'd dedicate more time to her garden, start the book she always wanted to write and, most importantly, call her friend Joanna, who was going through difficult times. One step at a time, that was her plan for today. Tomorrow, back to work where she could while away the hours without being beset by existential issues. Hopefully, she'd work till she died, as her husband had done. "Lucky him!" she thought, to have died before being forced to retire. And how could he retire anyway, if he was a writer. And he'd never run out of inspiration because he'd always had her, his main companion and solace. "Lucky bastard! I hate him! I hate him!" and finally she broke into sobs.

Tangled stories

Chapter One: Manuel and Nadia

"Let me know if you need something and I'll go and help you," Manuel had said, afraid of having sounded patronizing. She was a beautiful, humble girl and he didn't want to impose pseudo-disinterested help on her. He was afraid he wanted to see her much more than she was available and that would end up undermining their relationship.
It was raining with abandon and Manuel had decided to start a new book to stem the flow of his emotions before they swept away the precarious love nest they'd built. Busy-ness was the key to a healthy relationship, that and pretending that something besides her mattered to him. He'd just finished a book so it seemed he'd fallen in love again with impeccable timing. Every one of his books had been triggered by a raw experience of love that he had taken upon himself

to sculpt and polish, but this one, like the previous ones, was meant to last forever.

Manuel had been working on his latest article: On the origin of the Universe, and he'd found out that he'd been misinformed at school; he hadn't been taught Einstein's theory of relativity, which was simply enlightening. He was ever more embittered by Argentinean public education and he was ever surer to remain in Poland.

Relativity plus quantum theory, in their incursions into cosmology, had almost explained the whole universe; just a dose of philosophic speculation was needed to make them complete. There were still doubts about whether the universe was going to end in an implosion or whether it was going to expand eternally thus creating a new universe in its bosom. The theory of multiverses had been created, with parallel lives and other nonsensical ideas. Manuel thought that if there were parallel lives to his, he'd gotten the worst of it, so he was simply discontent with that kind of unjustified speculation; it didn't solve anything and it just added more layers of confusion. Manuel's spirit yearned to realize that it was unique and that everything it had done had some sense at least, and for this feeble hope to hold water he needed to dismiss the science-fictional terrorism that promulgated the existence of other realities. For his life to make any sense, he needed to exist in a single universe, where everything had some influence on his environment and on his own life. Parallel universes or afterlife utopias were simply out of the question for someone who wanted to take the reins of his life.

But how difficult was it going to be to take control of his life when he depended so much on someone else's decision: Nadia still hadn't made up her mind about him. She was a beautiful blond Polish girl with big eyes that emanated their greyish blueness from the whiteness of her face. Although she was attracted to Manuel and she would've surely given him a chance in other circumstances, the situation was a little complicated by the fact that she was married.

She was working in her flower shop one afternoon when Manuel
came in and instead of buying something, he just asked for
directions. An hour later he was back just to tell her that he'd found
the place and he thanked her; he also meant to buy a flower for
someone special and he asked her advice "What flower do you
consider the most beautiful of all?" he asked. She said, "I like lilies
the most" and she pointed to a white one. So he bought it and after
having paid, he handed the flower back to her and said, "It's for you"
in which she delighted, not so much for having been given one of her
own flowers as a gift but for the handsome face and refulgent dark
eyes of her suitor. She smiled and joked, "Thank you, my favorite
flower, how did you know?" to which he answered, "Because its
beauty matches perfectly with yours." After a brief conversation, he
left the shop, not without asking for her phone number.
Now when he texted her another of his romantic phrases, she was
making dinner for her husband. She loved her husband, but the
passion had long ago gone and she felt a withering in the bloom of
her youth. She'd married him at twenty and now she was only
twenty-two; they hadn't had a child yet because he wanted to have a
house big enough to accommodate three children before having the
first one. It was a peculiar algorithm, but she accepted her husband's
judgment on this matter because she wasn't so eager to have a child.
So when she read Manuel's trivial phrase, she saw a way out of the
stalemate situation she was in; she thought a little platonic love
could raise her spirits and even save her marriage. She answered
him, not without waiting the conventional amount of time before
texting back suitors, that is to say, four hours. Thus, passion could be
kept at a reasonable pace, reading and answering messages every
four hours. Thus, the flame of his desire grew exponentially while
she made sure she wouldn't be burned by it.
Manuel hated texting because he was a humanist and he saw with
bitterness how this telegrammic form of conversation took over our

lives. He was the kind of person who prefers sporadic misunderstandings to overcommunication. He was one of those people who like accumulating feelings for many days before writing a long and urgent love letter. But he'd been born in the technological era and, after being dissuaded from his letter-writing habit by his constant lack of success, he conformed to the general rule and started adapting his art to the meager capacity for expression he found in texting. So he, twenty-six by now, had mastered the art of letting the girl know you're interested without smothering her with uncalled-for effusions of emotions. The problem was that he had a remnant of strong emotions he needed to channel somehow. That's where writing came in; writing and occasional inconsequential romantic relationships. He'd been with girls he'd found sexy, although he wasn't in love with them, but those relationships weren't meant to last long. The moment he'd met Nadia he was demoralized by his lack of prospects for the future and he'd seen a new meaning to his life in her. He just poured out the emotion he'd felt on their first encounter in easy four-hourly installments; he had enough to go on writing for months because neither the cellphone screen nor his heart were big enough to contain all of his feelings. However, after a week of tense expectation, she agreed to meet him again.

Chapter Two: On the origin of the universe
"In the beginning was the Word, and the Word was with God, and the Word was God"- John 1:1.
The question of the origin of the universe is a philosophical question and not simply a scientific one. The origin of the universe is an ontological problem rather than a physical one. It's an existential question too because when we're looking at the origin of the universe, we're looking at the reason for existence. Out of a desire for scientific accuracy, being attached to the positivist ideals of a Western society, I tried to read about all the progress science has

made regarding this matter. But this is a theological issue rather than a scientific one and, more importantly, it's an existential issue. The Vedic philosophy says that in a drop of water you can see the universe; we can therefore compare the universe to a family: matter and anti-matter don't annihilate each other; they form new life: the same as a man and a woman form new life at the expense of their own vital energy.

The main problem with scientific theories is that they are reliant on mathematics. Mathematics is a great science that has allowed us to achieve great technological advances and feats of engineering, but it's useless to derive the meaning of things from the contemplation of our environment. Therefore, all the theories that confine the universe to a mathematical determinism are leaving aside the most important element in life: soul. And this term does not apply only to human beings but to everything that exists. Because there are only two possible options: either we believe that human beings don't have a soul and therefore they're determined by physical laws, like everything else in the universe, which implies that our spiritual and moral inquisitiveness is just pure entertainment while we wait for physical laws to dispose of us, or we believe that humans do have souls, which must come from somewhere and this somewhere is the whole universe. Therefore, all things that exist have Soul in them; everything is alive and conscious, from rocks to atoms, and the level of consciousness is the only thing that differentiates us from animals and plants. But what is the soul? And here is where we differ from religious conceptions; the soul is simply: consciousness. The only difference is that we're supposed to "lose consciousness" when we faint, when we sleep or when we die, while the soul lasts forever. However, there's no such distinction; because consciousness exists eternally, although in different states. When we die, it exists in a latent state until it's reembodied.

Here we see an ontological dualism between matter and

consciousness. There are different levels of consciousness in the world, and they're embodied in correspondingly evolved forms. Therefore, every conscious being is a galaxy. Why do I say we're galaxies and not universes? Because as galaxies, we're in contact with other galaxies and sometimes we can interact with them. If we were universes, we wouldn't feel the presence of things other than our own bodies. That's why I refuse to believe the idea of various universes. That's a mathematical shortcut scientists have chosen to take to obviate perceptional problems they found in their theories. There's just one universe; that's our determinism. That means that everything we do affects other people, our environment and, more importantly, determines our destiny.

Darwin has shown that we evolve, and this seems to be our nature. As a civilization, we're born brutes and we learn and enlighten ourselves; it doesn't happen the other way round: that we're first enlightened and then we become brutes. The problem is that our science collapses from time to time; there are moments in which we give up and there's a process of brutalization or regression. However, we never return to the previous point; civilizations evolve, even though insignificantly. Thus, we can say that we're more evolved than the Greeks in moral and spiritual matters, although insignificantly. A clear example is the family, where two enlightened people give birth to a brute, that needs to be enlightened also, but who, by the laws of spiritual evolution, will be slightly more evolved than the more evolved of the consciousnesses that coupled.

The Universe

Universe means, literally, that which is turned together, but, more importantly, it means a whole. Even if there were multiverses, which turned and behaved as separate entities, there would still need to be a correlation between them or no correlation at all; in the former case, we still would be talking of a universe, formed by different multiverses, and in the latter case, our universe would be totally independent from the other ones and therefore their existence would be meaningless to us.

Simple intuition leads me posit the idea of a single universe first. Enshrined in the concept of universality is the idea that a universe is independent, which means that the only point of contact it may have with other universes is in its genesis. Therefore, the key question is the origin of all existence, be it one single universe or multiple multiverses; from there we can derive a whole theory of universality or multiversality, whatsoever may be the case.

In the Rig Veda's cosmology, the god Vaak created the universe. Vaak is a Sanskrit word that means word or speech and it's the origin of our word "voice". Vaak is the god that "utters the Word of Truth" and therefore can be equalled to the Christian god: "God said, 'Let there be light'; He willed it, and at once there was light." Genesis 1:3-5. Because both Word and light are creators, both are generators of existence.

However, no religious text gives a satisfactory answer to the creationist question. The Christian and Muslim religions attribute it all to God or Allah, but the descriptions of the creation fail to explain everything science has discovered, as they are anthropomorphic theologies. The Rig Veda theology is more honest in its approach:

Who really knows, and who can swear,

How creation came, when or where!

Even gods came after creation's day,

Who really knows, who can truly say

When and how did creation start?

Did He do it? Or did He not?

Only He, up there, knows, maybe;

Or, perhaps, not even He.

— Rig Veda 10.129.1-7

We can see here a slightly less anthropomorphic theology, where there is the "suggestion" that there's a superior form of consciousness: "He", who may or may not have created the universe and may or may not have done it deliberately. All three theologies, as well as other ones that I haven't mentioned only for practical reasons, share the idea of a "superior consciousness". That's an intuition the most important religions and spiritual movements have had. However, no theology can be totally trusted, as they're man-made interpretations of existence and they were developed before most important scientific discoveries were made. The problem with religions is that they're generally moral constitutions on which societies are built and therefore amendments are difficult to make. They don't work like scientific movements, which are always subjected to changes of paradigms. Therefore, I took the sound ideas of every theology I came across and dismissed all the ideas that weren't sufficiently intuitive to me; for instance, the idea of Brahma as a creator in the Vedic cosmology, or the Christian idea of God as a creator, which would mean the universe is a trialism of God, matter and our consciousnesses or souls.

The human factor: consciousness
In the working of our brains, we see a feature that can be called selective memory or rather selective oblivion, which is more clearly seen in prodigious savants. Savants have extraordinary mental abilities which are the product of an arbitrary concentration of consciousness in a limited area of reality. A malfunction in their brains makes them remember things that normal brains are programmed to forget or leads them to develop specific mental abilities, generally related to mathematics. However, we all know that the most powerful mental abilities are reasoning and creativity and that all other mental functions can be computerized. Therefore, we may conclude that our brains are programmed to enhance these capacities, deliberately getting rid of useless information or abilities.

There's a part of our brains that selectively forgets irrelevant events and that hampers the development of some mental abilities that are ultimately useless to our spiritual development. If that's true for us in the course of our lives, it must also be true in the course of our eternity. That means that when we die, the information and abilities that are useless to our spiritual development are deliberately forgotten as we are reborn into the world.

Speed of light

The speed of light is absolute: 671 million miles an hour. That means that light cannot travel faster; it can't be influenced by the physical laws of relativity. Everything has a frequency; thus, everything can convey the idea of time, but when we move faster than the speed of light, then time stops. All matter stops moving and we'll live eternally as pure consciousness, without matter: that would be the nearest approximation to the Christian idea of Heaven or rather closer to the concept of Nirvana. However, there's a small flaw in the Christian conception. Consciousness does not like eternity; consciousness seeks an object to concentrate its energy on. Thus, consciousness will take up matter and be reborn again into its material existence. The key point here is that all consciousnesses will be united in one single consciousness because there's no barrier to divide them. Every consciousness will be omniscient and therefore omnipresent, and the only way to do this is to be one single mass of consciousness. However, there will be as many consciousnesses as there are particles in the universe. This number won't be infinite, but it will be unmeasurable. Because the time someone would take to measure this number at the speed of light wouldn't be long enough to count it all before a new universe would be created. Therefore, the conundrum of eternity is solved by a simple technical question: the inability to count to a certain number. Because if we're saying that time stopped, it's because we've reached an "infinite speed" which allows us to defeat the laws of matter which create time. The infinite speed is just a little above the speed of light. A single consciousness won't need to traverse the universe to be present everywhere, but it will be connected to the other consciousnesses and it will therefore feel what they feel and be wherever they are.

After an eternal time, which will actually be no time at all, all these consciousnesses will decide in unison to take up matter, which will bring about a new Big Bang. As every consciousness takes up a particle of matter, time will resume its course. However, consciousness will be annihilated as a whole because it's been divided into individual parts; it has been trapped in matter. Therefore, the force of matter, which is a contraction force and may be equalled to the gravitational force, will outbalance the force of consciousness, which is an expansion force and will not exist at this moment. In an infinitesimal moment, the universe will contract. This moment will not be infinite because the laws of matter will already apply; it will therefore be a moment equivalent to the phenomenon called the Inflation of the Universe. The universe will therefore "deflate", contract or have a big crunch, in whatever way we may call it, until the point where the laws of matter won't allow for further contraction. Then and only then, when matter has fused into a single particle, consciousness will wake up. Because, if we compare the universal consciousness to our own individual consciousness, we know that although we may hear sounds while we sleep, although we may sleepwalk or even talk and move, we aren't fully conscious until all the senses of our body are. Thus works the universal consciousness. Only when all the particles have been reunited, the consciousness as a whole can wake up. The consciousness is, however, formed by innumerable consciousnesses which have lost their memory of what has just happened and they seek to expand, as it's their nature. Thus, some consciousnesses will mingle together, which will actually annihilate the potential of the whole, but it's a natural process of evolution. They tend towards entropy, which means simply that consciousnesses tend towards "devolution" or "coupling" with other consciousnesses if they are not making a deliberate effort towards evolution. This is just a natural tendency of every being, and it's called the instinct of reproduction when applied to living beings. However, this characteristic is also seen in inanimate things as well as in basic elements. In human beings, it's sometimes channeled into activities such as teaching, writing or even simply speaking, where our ideas are reproduced. This process of devolution, which consists of sharing our spiritual knowledge, is more evident in sexual reproduction, which brings forth one or many new consciousnesses, which by the laws of spiritual evolution will be slightly more evolved than the more evolved of the consciousnesses which coupled. Thus, the partial neutralization of our consciousnesses, which is necessary to submit to the physiological act of reproduction, and the paternal instinct give rise to more evolved consciousnesses than ours. Then, when we die, we're "summoned" by the physical union of two consciousnesses slightly less evolved than ours and therefore we continue the cycle. In the hypothetical case that there weren't any couplings of two consciousnesses at our spiritual level, we would have to wait to be reborn into the world. Thus, we would exist only in latent form, because consciousnesses can't evolve without being intertwined with matter.

Chapter Three: Marina

Marina was always happy to see Manuel, although she didn't always show it. Since their breakup a year before, they'd managed to consolidate their friendship, but she still didn't know how to handle her emotions whenever she learned about his sporadic incursions into female territory. For Manuel had become so familiar to her that she couldn't help filling the gaps in the imaginary depictions of her future with his face. She felt irremediably attached to him, no matter what he did or said, and that was why she tried to change his life for the better.

Marina had come to Warsaw for work a year-and-a-half before; she'd graduated from the Universidad Autonoma de Madrid with a Masters in economics and innovation management. She was working for a Polish company, but she was paid as she would be back in Spain. She'd met Manuel at a party with lots of vodka and chips two months after her arrival. It was one of those parties at which there's little dancing and lots of drinking, and she wasn't feeling so comfortable being offered a vodka shot every fifteen minutes. After the first shot burned through her throat into her stomach, she started feeling sick and lonely. "You should eat something; it helps soak up the alcohol," was the friendly Polish advice she received, while being offered chips that made her feel sicker. She sat in a corner, trying to go unnoticed until her heartburn and her melancholy passed away.

She was doing well alone in her corner, when someone talked to her in Argentinian Spanish. "Funny accent," she thought. She'd never talked to an Argentinian before, although back in Spain it was full of them. "I'm Manuel," he said, "are you enjoying the party?" "He doesn't seem very perceptive," she thought, but she answered honestly, "I think vodka and chips are a terrible combination." "Me too!" he said, "I brought my own beverage." He grabbed a glass of wine from a nearby table and waved it in front of her. "You want a glass?" "No thanks," she said, "I'm going soon." "Would you like to dance before you go?" he asked, almost formally. She'd actually gone to that party with the intention to dance; she missed the wild nights back in Spain. Her stomach had already recovered and she didn't mind a little fun before she left; besides, her gonna-be dancing partner had sweet inquisitive eyes and a seductive smile that was quite encouraging.

They danced for half-an-hour in front of dazzled Polish eyes unaccustomed to seeing dancers stepping on the beat and hips moving in a graceful fashion, almost effortlessly. People paid specific attention to her hips, which, to everyone's surprise, had suddenly come alive. It was as if a bird had taken flight in the middle of the room; everyone was struck by the sudden event and looked hypnotized at the to and fro of her skirt. They danced heedless of their audience, each one focusing only on the person in front of them. Even by the time the novelty had worn off and the Polish people had stopped paying attention to the dancers, they went on entranced in their subtle game of seduction. When she came back to her senses, she remembered her previous resolve to leave the party so she said, "Thank you" and headed to the door. Manuel followed her and asked for her phone number, which she gave him, not for the purpose of answering his future messages but out of gratitude for having had a good time. Then he took her by the hand and said, "I think I was the only one who wasn't looking at your hips while we danced." "Really?" she said, "If everyone was looking at my hips, that makes me the only person who was looking at yours," and she smiled tauntingly. "I actually took a peek whenever I had the chance," he confessed, but he wasn't the kind of guy who knows how to seize the magic moment, so after seeing he hadn't planned on kissing her, she said goodnight and started walking away. However, Manuel was the kind of guy who is as persistent as a migraine, so after a few seconds, he raised his voice to say, "Can I walk with you?" "I'm taking a night bus nearby; I live downtown," she said. "That's OK, I also take the bus and I think the evening is over for me too."

Their conversation was quiet as the night; the residential area they were walking through was dimly illuminated, which allowed them to connect with the stratospheric world and the universe. A star had tangled itself in Marina's hair and Manuel was trying to untangle it, or that's at least what he said when he suddenly caressed her hair. The rest of the walk went by uneventfully, except for the events in their bodies, which were filled with fresh air and emotion. When they bid their final goodbye, he dared to kiss her slightly on the lips and she dared not to turn her face away. Thus, two foreign souls found a respite from their respective exiles.

Chapter three: Elio and Valentina

Elio had met Manuel and Valentina at the same weekly Italian meeting. He was sitting beside Manuel when he saw her enter and sit on a chair quite distant from him. After half-an-hour, he couldn't restrain himself any longer and he went over to her and, after introducing himself, he drew a nearby chair up beside hers and engaged her in conversation as only Italians know how to do. Valentina was a Ukrainian girl who had graduated in Italian philology, but she was now studying international relations because that would give her more chances of getting a good job. She was very nationalist, which implied a deeply rooted contempt for Poland, but she hadn't been able to go anywhere better till now so she was putting up with her current undesirable situation. Going to Italian meetings and talking to Elio was a treat for her, especially since he showed that he was interested in the details of her life and every opinion she had on even the most trivial matter. She enjoyed his lively conversation and the intensity of his eyes, as well as the undulations of his hair. She liked curliness; she found it manly. She told him about her plausible and implausible dreams, although she had to stop herself from divulging all her secrets in front of everyone around her.
She'd been born and raised in Kiev, but she'd moved to Poland to

experience more of the world. She loved her country and she wouldn't abandon it for anything in the world, but she wanted to be sure she knew enough about the world before settling down for good. Poland had seemed a very good idea at first, but now it started to bore her. The implicit discrimination against Ukrainian girls was evident; Polish girls were jealous of her beauty and they despised the fact that she came from a poorer country. She couldn't deny it was all true; she considered herself, indeed, prettier than most Polish girls, although back in Kiev she was outshone by many girls. Although she had a beautiful face, with big blue eyes and wavy blond hair adorning it, and although she had a slim body, she wasn't so tall, which put her at a disadvantage against taller Ukrainian girls. Back in Ukraine she'd resigned herself to her plainness, but here in Poland she'd just blossomed. The thin features of her face stood out from the round features of Polish female faces. Her almost inconspicuous curves and her thin legs were a sharp contrast to the general Polish voluptuousness and stoutness. She was considered attractive by most men and she enjoyed the new sensation.

But having an Italian suitor was the apex of her sexual fantasies; the Slavic temperament is romantic and passionate, but she enjoyed the rapturousness of the Italian character. She embraced spontaneity; she believed that foolish acts were worthier than brooding over what could've been. She knew there was only one chance for everything and she wanted to take every one of them. She wanted to live every moment and not to let an opportunity for happiness pass her by. So there she was, in front of a person raised in a carpe diem culture; she'd already started feeling the strong influence he was exerting on her. She was filled with enthusiasm and daring just by talking to him. While he talked, her minded lapsed into images of their elopement from sanity, their incursions into wilderness and bedsheets, and their constant flight from the oppressiveness of society. The feeling warmed her up and she found herself chattering uncontrollably. She couldn't restrain the pace at which she uttered her words; it was as if she were speeding in a car and she wanted to slow it down, but she couldn't take her foot off the accelerator. She was thrilled; she pressed down on that gas pedal and she let herself go at high speed. She knew she couldn't possibly maneuver herself to a normal speed, so she was just hoping that she would eventually run out of fuel.

The evening ended among smiles and deep silences on a walk home accompanied by him. He was a gentleman, so all his desire was expressed solely in his look. He kissed her goodbye on the cheeks and she started wondering about him. He was obviously attracted to her, but she wasn't sure about his intentions. She felt a partiality for him, but she had a sort of boyfriend back in Ukraine; actually, they were kind of planning to get married as soon as she went back. The poor guy had freaked out when she'd told him she was going to Poland for a year; they'd been together for a considerable amount of time, the amount of time that warrants a little concern when your partner decides to leave the country from one day to the next. He'd done everything but pull every one of his hairs out in a frenzy of anxiety. He'd been angry at first, then he'd implored, then he'd resigned himself to the fact that she didn't give a damn about his feelings and finally he'd opted for a proposal. She'd accepted because she was a conservative girl and he was her first man, which meant she was irredeemable in love with him. Everything would have seemed quite settled, were it not for her sudden urge to go abroad. However, she was a romantic person and she believed in love above all obstacles; maybe that was exactly the reason why she wanted to be separated from her lover: to test her theory of love.

All this sentimental baggage meant that she was less encouraging towards Elio than she would have been if she were totally free. However, the subtlety of this difference wasn't perceived by Elio, who wasn't so much concerned about these minutiae as he was concerned about getting her to like him better. So there they were, pulling from different sides, making strenuous emotional efforts which were ultimately meaningless. Because theirs was a strange equilibrium in which, no matter what they did, the sum of the forces would always equal zero.

Thus, they went on seeing each other, feeling and fondling each other, as is customary among people who suffer from a momentary loss of their sense of sight, generally called simply: being in love.

Chapter Five: Manuel and Nadia

They had been meeting for three months now and Manuel was on the verge of a nervous breakdown; he'd asked Nadia to ponder her feelings and make up her mind before their relationship started to wane. The problem of being in love is that our tolerance of "irregularities" seems to be dramatically lowered and that was the case with Manuel. He didn't mind going out with a married woman, for there wasn't any clause in his set of moral rules that prohibited it, but he couldn't allow the object of his love to lose his esteem. He couldn't allow her to be lukewarm when it came to love; he'd forced her to make a decision to save her from losing ground in his heart. Nadia had been to Manuel's place several times. It was the place they more frequently used for their encounters, because it was private and because they didn't meet very often and they felt the need to compensate for this with explosions of intimacy whenever they met. The first time she visited him, she saw a plant Manuel kept on the windowsill and remarked that the leaves were a little shriveled. She was afraid the plant would wither if Manuel didn't water it soon. However, she didn't tell Manuel about it; she wanted to see if he was capable of taking care of a plant. In their successive meetings at his place, she'd always check on the plant; sometimes she'd find it rejuvenated by recent watering and other times it was faded as a result of carelessness. The plant came to signify his reliability and she'd be a little gloomy whenever she saw the plant in bad shape. However, when Manuel asked her what was wrong, she'd never tell him it was about the plant because it wasn't actually the plant but Manuel that preoccupied Nadia.

Lately, the plant had shown signs of weakening irremediably to its death. Manuel seemed to have forgotten completely about the plant and she became more anxious every time she saw it; it had almost withered away when Manuel asked her to make up her mind about them. She didn't know what to do; by this time her heart was perfectly halved. One half belonged to her husband, for whom she felt immense gratitude and fondness, and the other half belonged to Manuel, whom she desired more than anything in the world. Sleepless hours she spent mulling over her situation, but she couldn't arrive at a definitive decision. Manuel had become restless and she saw, to her dismay, that his inner havoc had started to show up in his appearance. She didn't want to delay her decision any further, lest he hate her for making him suffer futilely. She decided to leave her decision to chance and to accept her lot as if it were written in Heaven. In that way, she'd never have to regret her decision because she'd made none; she'd just read the signals in the sky and followed the path they'd shown her.

However, as Sartre says, even when we think we aren't making our own decisions, even when we seek advice from someone and follow their advice, we're still condemned to choose; we can't escape this privilege. Because even when we've determined beforehand to follow someone's advice no matter what it is, the mere fact of having chosen their advice instead of someone else's is already a decision we've made. So if we go to a priest rather than to a liberal doctor when we seek advice about an abortion, we've already unconsciously made our decision. And that was the case with Nadia; she'd made up her mind even before she knew it, but she needed this "external factor" to soothe her conscience and tell her that she was less responsible for her decision, that it had been dictated to her and she had to submit to her destiny.

Nadia remembered the plant vividly; it was there as a symbol of her relationship with Manuel. Maybe it was her who had forgotten to water it; maybe it wasn't only Manuel's fault. But it wasn't the time to decide who was to blame; it was the time to assess the results of their being together and they weren't favorable. She'd lost all enthusiasm for her marriage and he'd grown low-spirited and melancholic; it hurt her to listen to the gloomy songs he sent her and to hear him talk despondently at times. She knew she was already making a decision when she decided on the symbol she would use to interpret her destiny, but she still held to the idea that magical things can happen and, like a Christian who prays to God for a miraculous sign of His existence, she was confident that a miracle would happen if it were her destiny to stay with Manuel.

She told him that she would have decided by the next time they met. Manuel didn't say anything; he was too anxious to think about whether she'd already made up her mind. He was a deeply spiritual person so he believed that every gesture, every single act of his would influence her decision. He was also a romantic person so he liked to believe that, even if she'd already reached a decision, he could convince her to be with him at the last moment, by saying or doing something that would make her see that they were meant for each other. However, he knew he wasn't able to bear the nerve-wrecking situation he was in for long, so he knew that he'd have to accept her decision, be what it may, and move on if she rejected him. He knew he'd forced a situation, that he could've waited a little more to give her time to get attached to him, but he also knew he had no strength left and that he needed to put an end to it all. The odds were against him and he knew it, but he was also waiting for a miracle to happen.

Nadia arrived punctually, as if destiny couldn't be postponed. Manuel had spent an hour looking for a flower that would mean love, but also understanding and friendship in case she decided to break up their relationship. It needed to be a lily because romance relies on symbolism and that flower symbolized his love. He'd first chosen a bright yellow lily that didn't have the bloody resolution of a red one, but then he saw a white one, which would mean passive acceptance of her decision and hope for the best. He picked the white one and went home to wait for Nadia. When she entered, he kissed her passionately, as if it were the last kiss he'd give to a woman, and handed her the lily. She thanked him with a kiss and laid the lily on top of her bag, which she'd left on the edge of the couch. She was looking downwards all the time, as if afraid to betray her feelings. Manuel was mute; he wanted to embrace her passionately, but he was paralyzed by fear; he could only stare at her and wait for her to make conversation or to tell him her decision at once. Nadia walked around the room and stopped at a certain spot, heaving with emotion. Manuel didn't know what to think and he approached her carefully. He saw that her eyes, full of tears, were fixed on the windowsill. She was looking at the plant that had suddenly bloomed and was as green as hope. She turned her watery eyes towards Manuel and told him, "I'm staying with you, Manuel. Destiny wants it thus."

Chapter Six: Marina

It had been around a year since Manuel had broken up with Marina. It wasn't easy to identify a specific date, moment or situation in which he'd drifted apart from her, which gave her also little hindsight on their relationship. Manuel was still a mystery to Marina, and until she could solve it, she wouldn't let go of him. However, the memories were too painful to try to forget about them. There they were, in her apartment; he'd stayed overnight on a spare couch she had. It was snowing hard and it was too late so, in spite of all his apprehensions, he'd decided to sleep there and get back home early in the morning. He'd been reading till late, long after she'd gone to bed. She knew it because she knew him; she knew he couldn't sleep when he was tense, and she'd felt he was at that moment. But why? She'd tried to make it seem natural; he'd already stayed over many times before; they'd practically lived together. Even after they broke up, he came sometimes in the evening – she always felt lonelier in the evening – and they read or watched something together. She'd sit beside him, maybe take him by the hand, sometimes even try to steal a kiss from him, which he'd never allow. But he'd never walk out; sometimes he reacted merrily to her sexual assaults, other times he tried to put on a harsh face and remonstrate, telling her that she endangered their friendship by behaving like that. She couldn't believe a friendship could be ruined by some physical contact, but she'd never tell him that. Because she still remembered that night, two weeks after he'd finally decided they couldn't be together, when he came to visit her and, after not much effort on her part, he'd kissed her passionately and had laid her on the bed to succumb to his repressed desire. She knew he was repressing himself in front of her; she knew he wanted to be with her as much as she wanted it. Even now, a year after their last effusion of love, she knew his passion for her still flickered somewhere hidden in him. But how to reach that place?

She went to him naked as the new moon, her paleness was a reverberation of the silent chants of the luminary outside the living room window. There he was, sleeping semi-naked as he always did. He'd asked her for some shorts and a T-shirt, but she had none that could fit him, at least none she hadn't managed to hide from him. He couldn't sleep in his own clothes; they were too uncomfortable and he didn't want to iron them the next day. He was already asleep; it was two am and he'd put down his book already, passing from the imaginary world of a total stranger to his own imaginary world. Sometimes Marina wondered whether he spent even four hours a day in the real world.

She drew closer to him; every breath she took was a hopeful vessel she sent towards him; every step she made was a battle she won against her fear. He was inert, but he was more dangerous than a wakeful assassin; he was quietly sleeping, but he could still pass judgment on her, and he did. She felt the wrongfulness of every movement she made towards him; she only moved her feet, but she felt that every part of her body was running towards him. Even her eyelashes seemed eager to reach him, to look at him from a closer distance. What a wretched moment that is in which we're in between two opposite situations, as she was right now: on the one hand, the joy of expectation, the hope his dormant impulses would finally be aroused, and, on the other hand, the fatality of a possible rejection. At the beginning, when she got out of her room, only four meters separated her from him, a distance someone normally would overcome in six or seven steps, in three or four seconds. But as she drew closer the system of measurement changed; now meters became feet, then inches. Now she had her own way of measuring her acceleration: inches per square her anxiety. In the new realm she found herself in, time lost its meaning. She didn't know whether she'd been there for some minutes or a full hour; she wondered whether time had stopped and whether she might be infinitely trapped in this transitory dimension. She forced herself out of her trance by slightly caressing her thighs; in that way, she realized she still had control over her motor abilities and, more importantly, that she was still sensitive to touch. When she reached the couch, and was near to his feet, she stopped to recap the purpose of her being there. She couldn't remember; her mind was blank. She started fumbling in her mind for a possible reason why she was there at that moment; she thought of the pleasure of seeing him sleep. But then she realized she was totally naked. She slept in her pajamas, so her nakedness must have a purpose; what could be a tenable reason for it? She thought of simple aesthetics; she considered herself beautiful and this beauty was set off by the moonlight. It was art; her encroaching upon his sleep was a mere expression of her beauty. But then, what to do next? How to culminate this performance? What could the closing act be? To retreat into darkness again? Impossible! That's not how Shakespeare would do it; that's not the way good plays are meant to end. And now she was aware she was putting on a play, as usual, as everyone does in every action of their lives, only that this play was her masterpiece. How to end a chef-d'oeuvre? What was the convention? She only knew two kinds of play: comedies and tragedies, and she was sure she didn't feel like being laughed at. But she was in front of him; would she just bring down the curtain on a truncated play? That was more than her aesthetically sensitive heart could bear. She decided on a dramatic closing act. She laid her hand on the sheets that covered him, then she moved it along his leg towards his pelvis. He was sleeping on his back, his head turned towards the back of the couch. When she reached her final destination he started; he'd felt the warmth of her hand through the sheets. He looked her in the eye; however, he didn't see her nakedness. His look was full of horror; her presence represented the threat of her imminence beside him. He kicked her away and she fled the room in shame and confusion; she'd given herself to him and he'd kicked her like a stray dog.

He probably hadn't realized he'd kicked her because he was half asleep. It hadn't hurt her physically, but it had marked her morally. It wasn't the kind of tragic ending she was looking for; it was rather an ill-timed comic effect that cut short the climax. She didn't feel like crying; she felt, most of all, ashamed. She couldn't be a Juliette anymore; she couldn't die in dignity at that moment. She was just a joke and her life was just a badly written satire, something that wasn't worthwhile remembering. The next morning she didn't tell Manuel what had happened that night. He remembered her having come to him, but he didn't remember having kicked her away. He decided to leave the mystery unanswered, or rather he came up with a very easy answer to it: she'd gone to the bathroom and she'd stopped at his bedside to watch him sleep. He wasn't even sure she'd seen him open his eyes and he thought he'd imagined the nakedness of her body, which he'd seen in a flash before shutting his eyes.

Chapter Seven: Elio and Manuel

The old friends met at a bar in downtown Bologne. Manuel had gone to visit Elio, who'd moved away from Poland three years before. They seldom talked, but when they did, it was as if time had not passed between them. The turmoils of youth were behind them; Manuel's appearance was that of a settled-down man, while a masquerade of passion was all that Elio had left.

"I'm old already, Manuel; life's not what it used to be. I chose beauty over personality. I know I would've been so much happier with that nice girl I used to go out with. Instead, I chose Valentina and now I'm just a lonely old man. I wasted the best years of my life on her."

"Don't say that because you're just ten years older than me. I'll start feeling old too."

"Let's say you aged better. You made the right decisions and now you're full of happiness. I'm sixty and I can't get a proper erection with Marta. She doesn't turn me on; I hate to say it but she's too old for me."

"But she's only forty-five! You're still quite a cradle snatcher."

"Yes, that's exactly the point. You see, if I was twenty, I wouldn't mind being with a forty-five-year-old, provided she's hot. I'd still be turned on and my excess of enthusiasm would make up for her lack of ... sap, but now I can't be turned on by anyone beyond their twenties. Even a thirty-year-old woman's wrinkles ruin my ...

appetite."

"I understand, but what about love? I mean with Ela it's not a sexual roller-coaster, but we have intimacy, which is what counts. I can lie down in bed with her, make an attempt at wild sex or just squeeze her tightly in my arms, but when I look her in the eye, she's always that girl full of life I've been lucky to meet. Youth is in the eyes, Elio."

"Maybe I'll give Marta a chance; she's a lovely lady. She's willing to take care of this old man that blames his impotency on someone else. I'm tired of being alone. I'm not the irresistible guy I used to be; after the divorce it's not been the same with girls."

"Well, but all of your good and bad attributes lose meaning when you meet the companion of your life. Then you can't account for that stroke of luck even if you consider only your good attributes and add to those all the good attributes you always wanted to have. It's just not fair that you're so happy and that's why you need to become a better person: to even out your karma."

"So when are you starting to even out yours?"

"I've already paid my karmic debt. Who paid for our last beers?"

"Come on, Manuel! Don't tell me that Ela's worth just a beer. I think you could buy me that Lamborghini I always wanted and you'll be closer to redeeming the soul you sold to some pagan gods for her to be interested in you."

"I'll buy you a bottle of good Fernet and you'll stop conjuring my creditors. Deal?"

"Deal, for now."

Chapter Eight: Valentina and Manuel

Many years had passed since Valentina had divorced Elio. She was already in her late forties and it had started to show in her face and the lines of her body. Manuel's age was concentrated in some strands of hair that insisted on being as white as snow, which made him look like a grizzly bear lost in the Arctic. Both of them had regrets, but most of all Valentina, who, during her whole life had no sooner made a decision than she changed her mind."

"I'm not saying that women are dispensable items which I use for the sake of literature and then throw away when they stop inspiring me. All that I'm saying is that there are other themes than romantic love in my books; I also want to depict the existential struggle of men in their effort to conform to reality. We seldom realize the inherent romanticism of poverty, and I don't mean penury but lack of wealth. The lack of something gives meaning to this something. When I was a baby, I got ill and I needed to have an operation. It was New Year's Eve and my parents spent it in the small room of a public hospital. My father didn't earn much at that time and he hadn't received his salary yet, so he had little money. He bought a cider and a package of crackers to celebrate with my mom. That's what I want to talk about in my books, this love for life and the irony of happiness, which is found in the moments of greatest struggle and suffering. Look Vale, I'm famous now. I earn a considerable amount of money for every new publication, which means that the more I write, the richer I am. And that's not what I want, because *più guadagno, meno arricchisco la mia vita*. I want to be hungry every day, to have something to yearn for, something to romanticize about. It's hard to be a romantic in the comfort of a fully furnished house, with no problems other than my incurable laziness. I mean that tragedy is sometimes an enriching experience, and I just meant to encourage you to accept your current situation as an opportunity for rejuvenation."

"It's easy for you to talk about tragedy, Manuel; your life's deprived of it. You can look at it from your aloof standpoint and take pleasure writing about it. We common people don't have that advantage. We wallow in the mud of our problems just because we can't stand their stench. We can't detach ourselves from our problems because we care about them; we don't have the privilege you have: your selective indifference.”

“You're right, Vale, but I did care despite myself sometimes and you know it. I cared about you, about your choosing to leave me and go back to Ukraine. Those stings still burn under my skin and they're my ultimate source of inspiration.”

“Well, but now it's too late to take back what I did. I've gone so far just to end up here, beside my past.”

“You've messed up your life and you know it; there are wounds you can't cover with a band aid. But from the moment you accept this fact, you can start your journey of redemption. We're old, Vale; passion has already been rubbed out of our skins. Now we need to pace ourselves to the new rhythm of life; a rhythm without the pangs of youthful passion.”

“Oh Manuel, I'd be so happy with you at my side at this moment of my life.”

“Maybe, but you haven't earned the right to my company in my old age. You haven't quenched my youthful passions and now I don't feel grateful towards you. I need to be consistent at this time of my life. Now that physical attraction doesn't play a main role in my life, I draw happiness from the fact of being fair. And it's fair for me to give all my love to Ela, who's put up with my passionate selfishness for so many years. I hope you understand.”

“I know Manuel; I was just expressing my feelings. I hope Elio has already forgiven me.”

“He hasn't, but that's his problem. You've already paid part of your karmic debt and maybe you still owe some dividends, but that doesn't concern Elio anymore; it concerns only you. Remember that happiness is to be found in the lightening of our karmic burdens, and you have all the capacity to be happy now. Maybe loneliness is what you deserve, but also what you need right now.”

“I hope not. I can't be alone or I'll die. Promise me you'll always be nearby.”

"I'll always be nearby Vale; you're a meaningful part of my life."

Chapter Nine: Marina

Marina never said a word about that shameful night when she was kicked out of the room by Manuel; as with many things that happened between them, it was relegated to a private place in her memory.

She had met a guy in a disco where she'd gone for a friend's hen party. The guy was called Szymon and the night they met they had clicked, but she didn't seem to find a way to fall in love with him. She felt a heaviness in her heart whenever she drew too near him; it was as if she were betraying her freedom, a freedom she'd already surrendered to someone else. They corresponded by email and texted each other frequently, and they would talk for a long time on the phone, but from time to time she felt the need to reassert the boundaries between them and she didn't answer his calls or his messages.

He'd gallantly kissed her on the cheeks and she'd kissed him back on the mouth, but she always regretted it as soon as she'd done so; she felt ridiculous and she excused herself. Once she'd written him that she wanted to be just friends and he'd asked her to take it less seriously, just because he wanted to give her time to gather her thoughts. But the second time, he couldn't bear the connotation of her message; she wrote him that he'd asked her not to take it seriously so she was taking their relationship lightly. He knew she wasn't taking it lightly, but he felt she was testing him. Her message implied that he didn't want a serious relationship, which filled him with rage. He knew his rage was out of place, but he couldn't help it. He felt tricked into admitting to something he hadn't said, which would happen if he didn't say anything. Because she wasn't asking him but simply asserting the facts, so now he'd have to go back on his words or assume indifference to the status of their relationship.

He hated gratuitous drama and therefore he hated her at that moment, but he didn't want to lose her in a fit of passion, so he thought of her gentleness and attentiveness while he let the fury pass. Then he wrote her simply that it was serious for him, that he didn't play with such things and that he'd meant that she should take her time to decide. Now she had no way out other than taking it upon herself to make a decision about her future. She had no more excuses for her unhappiness; she'd found someone she cared about and he reciprocated her care and attention, but she still couldn't resign herself to giving up that which she did not possess: her heart.

Days became weeks and eventually a month passed before she could summon the courage to address her feelings. Szymon hadn't importuned her with messages or phone calls since his peremptory demand to make up her mind about what she wanted from him. She didn't want it to end like this, but she didn't want to submit herself to an emotional charade just to appease his hurt feelings. She wanted to build on sincerity so she texted him: "Hi Szymon, how're you? I'm sorry for not writing sooner; I thought carefully about your demands and expectations and I can't fulfill them, so I wouldn't like to hurt you more than I already did. I can just apologize to you and hope you'll forgive me. I appreciate your friendship, but I can't enter into a relationship right now. I ask you to consider me only and exclusively as a good friend, which I'll gladly be as long as I live. If you feel like not seeing me again, I understand, but if you want to talk to me some day, you don't need any excuse to call me. Take care."

Szymon read the wrenching text all at once, as if it were a shot of vodka he had to drink. His stomach burned for hours and he couldn't sleep that night, but the next morning his mind had forged the perfect answer. He texted her back: "Marina, long time, a piece of eternity I'd say, but I'm glad you wrote. We'll be whatever you want us to be; I have no power over you or over my destiny. I could try to tear myself away from you by artificial means, but I prefer to let it be what it must be. I appreciate your friendship too, so let's build on that."

It took them a while to enforce the law they'd enacted. There were some practical questions to solve before they could meet purely and exclusively as friends, but in the end their eagerness to see each other overcame their mutual apprehensions and they met fearlessly but still respectful of the covenant into which they'd entered.

Chapter Ten: Manuel and Nadia

Their year together had been like a prolonged honeymoon. He woke up every day wondering in which life he'd earned the right to be with her. But as the moon waxes and wanes, their romantic limbo started to recede and give way to everyday concerns. He went back to his writing and she went back to business. Their lives intersected only in the evening and at bedtime; besides that, they lived totally independent lives. He was a romantic person, so he didn't need more than an illusion to be in love, but she was a practical woman and she didn't feel the relationship was solid enough for her.

For a deceitful woman, she was quite trusting. She'd left her Facebook open on her laptop and he, distrustful as he was, had checked it. He was looking for a telltale message and he found it; it actually seemed to have materialized from the apprehensions in his mind. After that flirtatious message, he saw another one, this time from her, encouraging her suitor's boldness. Then he saw a time and a place; she was going to meet him the next afternoon in a secluded cafe. Manuel had anticipated such behavior on her part. He was romantic and he believed in love, but he was also pragmatic and he knew her weaknesses, which he loved as much as her strengths. If he hadn't loved her so much, he wouldn't have done what he did next, but he knew he didn't want to lose her and that he had to swallow his pride to keep her by his side.

The evening dragged interminably and he couldn't sleep that night.

She asked him if something was wrong and he blamed his sleeplessness on his stomach. "Probably the kielbasas I ate this afternoon," and he went to the living room with the book he was currently reading. At four am, his eyes started feeling heavy so he lay down on the sofa. The alarm woke him up at seven; only three hours sleep, but he felt more energetic than ever. It was as if he were in a battle; adrenaline didn't stop rushing through his veins. At work he couldn't focus; it's amazing to think how much time we can waste thinking about a single thing. By the time he realized, half the day was gone; the rest of the time he spent trying to do the minimum daily work so as not to get fired.

He went back home, took a quick shower and lay down on the sofa. It was five pm and Nadia was supposed to meet the guy at seven. Still an hour-and-a-half to go and he couldn't do anything but think of the possible scenarios after he did what he was going to do. The worst result he could get was that she'd be upset because he followed her and she would leave him for the guy. She could also just get upset over what he was going to do, but also stop seeing the other guy, which still gave him a chance to recover her. She could be too ashamed to be upset and her relationship with the guy could prove to be nothing but an impulse that would die that same afternoon. In the best of cases, she'd realized he loved her and she'd never do it again. An hour passed and he decided to go there before anyone else, so he could find the best place to hide. He arrived at the cafe half-an-hour earlier, but rather than going in he found a suitable place to stand without raising suspicions and which provided him with a view of the entrance. He went for a walk so as not to attract anyone's attention and he came back fifteen minutes later. Now he stood there, pretending he was texting and sometimes calling someone on his phone. It was ten minutes past seven and he started to get nervous. He decided to wait for ten more minutes and then go in and search for them. At last he saw her entering the place; she was elegantly dressed, nothing too provocative; she didn't need it to be sexy. He waited for ten more minutes; he wanted to make sure both would be there. When his impatience was greater than his common sense, he went into the cafe. He walked in carefully, so as not to let the prey escape. When he had scanned the whole of the first room, he sat down at an empty table to take a look around again and make sure they weren't there. He passed onto the next room and after a quick scan, he saw them. Fortunately, they hadn't seen him, but he wanted to use the surprise factor on them so as to have a greater effect. As he got closer, he saw the guy was taking her hand; she was sitting with her back to the entrance so she couldn't see him and the guy probably didn't know him yet. When Manuel got to the table he caressed her shoulder and said, "Nadi", giving her a soothing look. She stood up by instinct, as if trying to escape being caught sitting with a stranger. She said, "Manuel, this is Piotr. Piotr, this is my boyfriend Manuel." The guy concealed his surprise very well and he stretched his hand towards Manuel, but something in Manuel's eyes made him forget about that idea. "Are you ready to kill for her?" he said, and not leaving any time for the question to sink into his interlocutor's mind, he added, "Because I'm ready to die for her." Manuel saw Nadia from the corner of his eye; she was too shocked to say or do anything. He gave one step forward towards his prey and grabbed him by the collar of his shirt and twisted the cloth until it almost strangled the guy. "Next time I see you with her, I'll die or kill," he said, making use of all of his creole savageness to give emphasis to his message. The guy hadn't moved an inch; he was counting on Manuel not making a scene in a public place. Manuel was beyond caring about etiquette, but there wasn't anything else to do. He'd made his point clear and he didn't want to destroy china or expensive glassware. "Don't even dare to look at her," Manuel said when he released his hold on the guy, who was taller and better built than him, but less interested in a fight to the death. Piotr just lowered his eyes and walked away, while Manuel followed him with his eyes till the entrance. Then he took Nadia's hands, which were restless, and he kissed her cheek. He didn't have any energy left, not even to reassure her that he still loved her, but she understood and she wrapped herself in his arms. The people who'd been watching with interest now started diverting their glances from the couple, so as to give them some privacy. Manuel collapsed on the chair in front of him; the tiring day added to the strenuous emotional effort he'd just made had just exhausted him. Nadia caressed his head while he recovered; then she guided him home, leading him like a blind person through the streets. They arrived home; they were safe now and Manuel felt sure that nothing else would ever dare threaten their love.

Chapter Eleven: Elio and Valentina

Valentina needed to go back to Ukraine to finish her masters degree. It was going to take at least six months for her to do it, so Elio started to brace himself for her absence. Valentina looked rather excited to be going back to her family; she felt uprooted in Poland. On the day of her departure, Elio promised to go and visit her at least twice a month, a promise which he wouldn't be able to fulfill because of various excuses Valentina would make whenever he was ready to go to Kiev. He was consoled by the idea that she was trying not to waste time so as to come back as soon as possible, but when the semester was over and she didn't show any sign of coming back to Poland, he started to despair.

Valentina had finally found herself in Kiev; she felt her life was going at the pace she wanted for once in her life. She thought of Elio every day, but she couldn't make herself leave her life in Kiev. In the meantime, she met her ex-boyfriend, who'd broken up with her to pursue his dreams in the United States. He'd come back six months before after having finished his two-year pilot course and now he was working for the Russian Air Force. Valentina wasn't aware of the fact that she'd actually timed her period in Poland so as to coincide with the time her ex had spent abroad. Now that both of them were back, there was a feeling of common destiny in the air and she couldn't help but be aware of it. He didn't show indifference to her either. He'd broken up with her for practical reasons and, although he hadn't missed her in the United States, he was glad to know that she was still available and well-disposed towards him. They resumed their amorous encounters, which evolved into a fully fledged relationship whose only possible outcome could be marriage. And so they married, in a way that was untimely but not unexpected; he, encouraged by the euphoria of being back in his fatherland, with a degree and a promising job; she, leaving aside all her career plans and previous commitments. Theirs was meant to be a nirvanic state in which everything else ceases to exist, and so it was, as regards Valentina's relationship with Elio. He only realized that she was married when he saw the pictures of the wedding on her Facebook wall. Valentina had unconsciously hoped that the gravity of the situation would be so overwhelming that Elio would just accept the fact painlessly, or at least that he'd quietly withdraw his intentions of being with her. Elio did the latter, but he failed to do the former. He was so upset by the news that he couldn't even muster the courage to ask her what it was all about. He knew she owed him at least an explanation, but he felt as pathetic as a bug asking the man that's going to crush it with his foot why he's doing that. He had only one certitude; he meant nothing to her, and he didn't want to dwell on it. He chose oblivion rather than outrage; he chose to move on rather than to demand an explanation that would lead to nowhere.

Months later, Elio could breathe and eat, even sleep without images of Valentina crossing his mind. For all practical purposes, Valentina was dead to him and she'd never come back. The fact that she lived in another country was really convenient because the ghost of her presence didn't haunt him. Ukraine was the ninth hell, according to his own interpretation of Dante's Inferno, and, provided he didn't descend to hell due to his sins, he'd be safe from her. His overt Italian nature and attractive features made him pleasant to the eyes and ears of other Polish girls, who didn't delay in falling madly in love with him, as if investing themselves with the Italian passion that they'd seen in movies. Elio wasn't ungrateful for these shows of affection towards him, and his complacent nature obliged him to give all those girls a chance until he was completely sure he wasn't in love with them. He never found the same madness he'd found with Valentina, but he found nicer and even prettier girls than her. In the end, he realized that his love for Valentina had been simply a reflection of all his fantasies, which had now been dissipated to make space for real love, based on companionship and selfless help, the kind he was developing now.

Destiny wanted it that they saw each other again years later, and this immediately brought to Valentina's mind a remembrance of what could've been. By then, Elio was in a happy relationship and Valentina had too many regrets to think that not having abandoned Elio would've made any difference in her life. But she remembered his kindness to her and she couldn't stop a wave of emotions from clogging her throat. She managed to say hi to him, as he stared speechlessly at her. He was as kind as he'd always been to her and that just made her break down in tears. He treated her as he'd treat a strange woman who's crying in front of him: he rubbed her arm and told her, "Everything will be OK, please don't cry, Valentina." She broke into a deluge of tears and wrapped herself in his arms. She didn't regret not being with him; she didn't think anything special about him nor had she any feelings for him. But she regretted her selfish behavior and for the first time she thought that, had she behaved less recklessly, she may have had a chance of being happy.

Chapter Twelve: Manuel and Nadia

Manuel and Nadia had gone to see a play called In Search of the Lost Time. It was a minimalistic play, with no more than two actors. It was performed by an amateur theater company; however, it was a lucid representation of the concept of time, and it became imprinted on Manuel's mind for years to come, especially this dialogue between the actors:

Henri : Hi Marcel, have you found my time?

Marcel : What? What time?

Henri : My time, I lost it.

Marcel : When did you lose it?

Henri : Exactly ...

Marcel : Think, Henri, think! It must have been around … What were you doing when you lost it ?

Henri : Exactly …

Marcel : That's it, Henri! You were probably doing something else and you just left it somewhere without paying attention.

Henri : You're right.

Marcel : So it must be somewhere around then. Try to remember the last thing you did.

Henri : I came to your place.

Marcel : So you must have lost it on the way to my place then.

Henri : Exactly! Thanks, Marcel. I've just found it.

Marcel : I'm glad to have been useful.

Henri : Believe me, you are.

During their walk back home, Manuel couldn't help mulling over the meaningfulness of that play's message in his own life. He'd lost so much time so many times, but wasn't he losing time at that moment? He wasn't sure and that ate away at him. Uncertainty was the symptom of unhappiness in his case; he knew this deeply inside himself. For a few days, he tried to elucidate what the cause of his unhappiness might be, but he also knew the answer to this question deeply inside himself. He wasn't in love with Nadia anymore. He'd fallen in love with her, but also with the romantic idea of the couple they formed. She'd fissured that idea a short time before and now it was starting to crack. Manuel could forgive, but he couldn't stop being an idealist. He still felt attracted to her, but the spasms of orgasmic pleasure had become just an animalistic activity to him and his heart wasn't developing anymore, nor was his soul expanding any further. He felt hampered by her, by her pragmatism, by her lack of ambition love-wise. He just walked out one night, leaving his clothes, his utensils and his belongings at her place. He just put on his best clothes and jacket, took his laptop with him and walked away from her flat. He explained everything that needed to be explained by SMS or Facebook. He even answered her calls and put up with hours of emotional vagaries from her. In the end, when her emotions had settled, he was able to send someone for his belongings, and they parted the best of friends although he never made a single effort to speak to her again.

During this time of crisis, Manuel was at a loss what to do next. He stayed at a friend's for a week, till he found his own flat. One night he just started walking determinedly but sadly, as if resigned to a well-known destiny. He walked through the city until he arrived at the street Nowy Świat; there he turned into another street and then another, looking always at the name of the streets on the signs, trying to find the one he was looking for. At last he found it, and he walked to the correct number. He rang. The gate just opened. He ascended the stairs and he rang again. There was a hubbub behind the door. There was a noise of women shuffling and whispering orders to each other. When the door was opened he saw women emerging from two doors and a hall; first there appeared old women and after, almost hidden from sight, young and supple ones. He saw her, the same girl he'd seen six months before when he'd come to the same place looking for some company; she had black hair and eyes, a generous bust and heavenly hips. Her glance was warm and distrustful at the same time, but this time her eyes glistened when he looked at her and said "Can I go with you?" She answered, "Yes, you're welcome" and led him to her room, the same room he'd been to six months before.

He didn't think she remembered him and, besides, he had other things on his mind to care about at that moment. He was making an unconscious effort to get Nadia out of his mind. Maybe the girl had raised her fee lately or maybe she'd just realized he was a little drunk, but, after refusing her offer, he simply said, "I only have one-hundred-and-twenty zloty", the exact amount he'd paid the last time. He didn't expect to find her there; he knew there were lots of girls and he knew he needed to forget Nadia; he didn't care about the means provided it was effective. He generally didn't enjoy sex for longer than fifteen minutes, after that he just went on for the girl's sake. So it was a real waste for him to be there because the minimum rate was for an hour's service, which left him a margin of forty-five unused minutes. In his love performances with girlfriends, he'd lasted even half-an-hour, but it was all out of love and his desire to please the girl he was with. But, knowing that he was paying the girl this time, he didn't feel inclined to last longer than his desire required. However, he made the effort to make his pleasure last longer while considering it an exercise for future performances with girls he was in love with.

During the twenty-five minutes he spent in the room with the girl, he didn't think of Nadia; the girl on top of him was so sexy and pretty that he would've married her if they'd been in a hotel room and she hadn't taken money from him. He said, "you smell nice", to which she answered smiling, "Thank you, but please focus." He finished earlier than expected and she went on moving until he had to stop her because it had already become dull. She cleaned him, which she hadn't done the last time, and he felt she was nicer this time. Last time, she'd looked suspicious and a little tense, but now she seemed at ease with him. She went to the bathroom and when he was dressing, she said, "You've visited us before, haven't you?" "Yes, I was with you," he said, and he saw an involuntary smile drawn on her face. "What's your name again? I forgot." "Nikola," she said and she glanced at him amiably, as if expecting him to say something more. He just smiled back at her and their love session was over. Physical love, like everything else, can be sold and, at a desperate time, when Manuel most needed it, he didn't care about the means by which he got it.

Chapter Thirteen: Marina

Szymon was made from chivalrous matter. He showed himself to be an inveterate monogamist, even when he didn't posses the object of his love. This excess of kindness had undermined Marina's reticence until she found herself in tears. Manuel's image came automatically to her mind, as it had come thousands of times, almost every single day since they last saw each other. Their conversation had stopped being passionate and just become amiable and playful, but this playfulness had maintained her hopes for the whole year in which they hadn't been together. They'd met, sometimes by chance and sometimes by arrangement, and she felt as in love with him every time as she'd felt when he first kissed her. Now he was simply an image that had started to get distorted in her mind. Where she had seen romance and passion before, now she saw cowardice and detachment. His kindness, which she'd considered a token of his love until now, had just become a memory to divert her during his absence. Tears of despair swelled her eyes. She cried out of impotence, then she cried out of pain then out of nostalgia. Finally, she was sedated by her sorrow. She was calm. She was at peace. At last she'd buried her impossible love.

He who doesn't know how to wait doesn't know how to rejoice. Romanticism does not mean creating an intricate plot that will eventually join the lovers; romanticism is a love story as simple as meeting someone in a bar and being honest enough to consciously fall in love with them. Here love is not a happy ending but a painful beginning. The couple will then have all the problems couples have, arguments, a few estrangements, but they'll never changed their minds about each other. For in the world of romance all the spasms of love happen after love is achieved, before it there are no real revolutions. For romance is not for the faint of heart, and only dutiful forbearance may conquer it.

And that was the case with Marina and Szymon. She drew her face closer to his a couple of times; she placed her hand on his lap and grabbed his hand delicately but firmly enough for him to see her new intentions. It took him three meetings to realize the change that had happened in her, but it didn't take him more than a second to agree to it once he saw it. It was the event he'd been waiting for and he was as prepared as a child can be when it comes out of its mother's womb. He was prepared for life and he cried, like a newborn, once he got back home. He cried without regrets, with childlike innocence, and then he just laughed and thought of the future ahead for him and Marina.

Marina, on her part, was in a state of simple joy. Her mind was at ease and her heart was in one piece again. Now that she could unchain her pent-up passion and feelings, she felt powerful and free. She breathed the same air, but she breathed it differently. The only thing that remained intact from her previous self was the gladness she felt in Szymon's presence; everything else was tinged with a different color and had a newborn meaning to her.

When I hear the … silence … of the world in a hurry, and I look at myself … in silence … in the reflection of so many eyes, and life hushes … in the silence … of a whisper, and it lulls me … silently

… until I fall in peaceful … silence.

Chapter Fourteen: A flashback from Manuel's romantic life.

Manuel was looking at the eyes in front of him; were they green, yellow or blue? He couldn't know with certainty. For a moment the darkness of a pair of brown eyes he'd seen with the same intensity back in Argentina came to his mind. That girl's beautiful features and the slenderness of her body had attracted his attention from the first time he saw her, but also her outspokenness that bespoke vitality. It was the same vitality he was seeing in the eyes in front of him now; these were kinder eyes, more attentive and quiet, but in their quietness he saw deep interest in him. The Argentinean girl was around fourteen and he was around sixteen when they met; back then his idea of a relationship with a girl was based on fairy tales in which he was supposed to be the beast and the girl was supposed to be the chaste beauty. He wasn't ready to look directly at female desire, and when he finally did, he was dazzled by it.

It was some months after he'd first met that Argentinian girl. They'd never spoken alone; he couldn't have found words to speak to her even if he'd had the chance. Basically, he adored her, not in the meaningless sense that this word takes nowadays, but in its real sense: he considered her divine, and he thought he could be redeemed by her; all of his apprehensions and his incurable timidity would vanish with an encouraging word spoken by her. But the fear of rejection was so great that he preferred to dream about her and to possess the idea of her love for him than to actually try to realize this love.

Probably she'd read his feelings from the way he looked at her and the way he spoke to her whenever they happened to exchange some words. There was a girls' meeting at his friend's house. His friend's sister had invited her schoolmates to watch a movie and his friend had invited him; they were the only boys at that meeting and Manuel felt a little awkward because of that. Her name was Erica, and she had just cut her finger that morning; she showed him the wound and he caressed her finger as if he were consoling a crying child. She smiled at him and he was glad his naivety had brought a smile to her face. He managed to sit beside her during the film and in the middle of it she searched for his hand. His heart beat violently while he grabbed her hand and put it into his jacket's pocket. Then she laid her head on his shoulder and he found it extremely difficult to remain immobile while a strong rush of emotions convulsed his whole body. They were surrounded by people and he was very shy, so he couldn't react. To aggravate the situation, his friend, who was sitting beside him, stared at him and said, "Comele la boca," which literally means "Eat her mouth", but which stands for a less radical action: To kiss her. He couldn't and he wouldn't make out with her in front of people. Maybe out of mere shyness, but also because his idealistic views on romantic love told him that to kiss a girl in public could blemish her honor. They just finished watching the movie in silence, only broken by the urgings of his friend to kiss her, and at the end of the movie a girls' chat ensued, giving him no chance to talk alone with his lady.

It was clear to him that she was already his lady; there couldn't be any possible doubt about that. And she was a brave one, not like the passive princesses of all the stories he'd read but a valiant princess that had dared to take her prince's hand and rescue him from his insecurities. But his illusion didn't last long. While his friend was walking him out of the house, he told him that she had a boyfriend. He dismissed the matter as something irrelevant and he encouraged Manuel to show her what it was like to be with a real man. He told him he was sure she'd leave that clown for him; he just needed to be firmer. But Manuel didn't share his friend's ideas; he was simply overwhelmed by the circumstances. He made a strenuous effort to understand why she'd do that, why she'd show interest in him if she had a boyfriend. He couldn't and he wouldn't analyze the situation until he talked to her, so he begged his friend to let him know when she was going to his house again.

Three days later his friend called him to let him know she was in his house. Manuel took his bike and rode there as fast as he could. He left the bike in the front yard and knocked at the door. She opened it. She feigned surprise when she saw him, which filled him with hope: she'd been waiting for him. There were only four people in the house that time: him, his friend, his friend's sister and her, but he still couldn't find a way to talk alone with her. However, his friend, who wouldn't see Manuel sink in front of his eyes, told Erica in front of him, "Manuel wants to speak with you; do you want to or *te cagás*?" which literally means "you shit yourself", but which is simply a more colorful way to say: you don't dare. Unfortunately, the girl was obviously well-versed in this kind of bullying so she answered "*me cago*", which, let's simply say, means: I don't dare. However, a short while later, she went up to Manuel and told him, "Do you want to speak?" and she walked towards an empty room, where she sat on a table. Manuel sat beside her and she put her hand on his lap, as a way to encourage him to speak. But he felt the need to make small talk, to create an affable atmosphere before touching upon the delicate subject. So, in a feeble attempt to make her feel at ease and summon up courage to ask her what he wanted to know, he asked her about her classical dancing and other things he knew about her life. But when Manuel realized that it was going to be impossible to ease into the real subject, he just said, "You're very pretty, you know." To which she answered, "Thank you." And then he said "So … you have a boyfriend?" To which she answered, "Yes, and I love him." At that instant her sister came to look for her and she fled away.

If only the Spanish saying were true and that scene in Manuel's romantic life had passed "without pain or glory", but it wasn't. There was no glory, but there was the martyrdom of thinking that he could've had her, only if he'd been braver and maybe tried to kiss her, or if he simply hadn't mentioned her boyfriend at that moment. And now he was in front of another girl that made him feel the same. He knew about female desire by now and he knew he couldn't expect them to be sleeping beauties that would be woken up only by his kiss. But Valentina had just shown him a new shade of female character. She'd just said she was really attracted to him and she liked him very much, but she loved her boyfriend back in Ukraine. And he didn't know what meaning the word love had for her; he just knew from experience that most people use that word to mean that they really want something. So she wanted to be with that guy and she called it love, and probably she mixed her desire with a sense of responsibility. Manuel didn't know; he just knew that he wasn't going to hinder love, whatever it might be, so he just told her, "Then I think we shouldn't see each other again." And she showed offence in her face and told him, "OK. Goodbye."

On his way back home, Manuel remembered another scene from his life in Argentina. He'd gotten drunk at a party and he didn't remember what had happened in the last part of the night. So he went to his friend's house and his friend told him the whole story. The most remarkable part was when they were dragging him to his friend's house and Manuel saw Erica's house. He asked them to stop and he grabbed the bars of the gate. Then he shouted, "Erica, you're the most whorish girl I've met in my life!" Manuel was paralyzed when he heard that and, to aggravate his misery, his friend had invited Erica over, mentioning to her that Manuel was there. Manuel only knew she was coming at the moment she appeared behind him on the sidewalk in front of his friend's house. Manuel couldn't even look at her, but that just augmented her intrigue. His friend took over and started retelling the story of Manuel's drunken feats, most of which were hilarious. Manuel hoped with all his heart that his friend would skip the part where they passed in front of her gate, but his

friend had actually strategically left it to the end. When his friend
mentioned the part in which Manuel saw her house and said, "Wait,
wait, wait, give me five minutes," Manuel glanced at the girl beside
him to try to guess what kind of sadist would want to tell her
something so atrocious. Then he looked back at his friend, and while
he mentioned the shout, Manuel unconsciously shut his eyes tight as
if trying to vanish by magic. But he heard some words that didn't
match the real story: "the most beautiful". His friend had twisted
Manuel's words to his advantage and now the product of his drunken
passion for her had been: "Erica, you're the most beautiful girl I've
met in my life!" She beamed with delight and Manuel wished for
that moment to last forever, but a couple of days later his friend's
sister told her the truth. Fortunately, he wasn't there when that
happened. "Are they green, yellow or blue?" thought Manuel, but he
couldn't make up his mind how to define Valentina's eyes.

Chapter fifteen: Manuel and Valentina
Valentina had just come to Poland and she'd joined the Italian group,
which Manuel had created on Facebook. He welcomed her in a
private message and asked her what she was doing in Poland and
how long she was staying. She said she'd graduated in Italian
philology back in Ukraine and now she was studying journalism and
had come on a student exchange program. She couldn't come to the
meetings, which took place during the week, so he told her they
could meet any time she wished, if she wanted to practice her Italian.
He found her beauty very different from the Polish beauty he was
already used to. Her face and body were different from the
characteristic Polish plumpness and her features were angular and
slender, not rounded as he generally saw in Polish girls. He'd already
seen other Ukrainian girls before and he believed them to be prettier
than Polish girls, especially since all the Ukrainian girls he'd met had
blue or green eyes and almost all of them were blond. He was really

excited when they met and he succeeded in convincing her to go to dance together on a Tuesday evening. She was a really conservative girl, just like the ones he'd met back in Argentina, and her manner was very different from the Polish style. When he tried to pull her towards him during the dance she resisted and, after a few tries, she said she couldn't dance closer because she had a boyfriend. Manuel didn't like that news at all, but he still harbored the illusion that she'd change her mind. He didn't have time to be anxious about it because she left for Ukraine three days later. She came back two weeks after that and they met in a park. She'd brought him some Ukrainian chocolates and, once they sat on a bench, he pulled out a rose he'd hidden behind his back and gave it to her. He didn't dare to stir the delicate topic of her boyfriend or his feelings for her, so the meeting ended without pain or glory.

The next time they met he was very straightforward; he got closer to her and wrapped his arm around her shoulders, not in an erotic way but to make a point, to show possession. He knew it was the worst possible strategy, since he knew that girls shun overt manifestations of feelings, but he'd lost all his patience already as he didn't know whether he was wasting his time on her or not. But he didn't say anything; he just kissed her cheeks until she reacted.

"What does this mean," she said, as a charming complaint. He hesitated for a moment. "It means I like you so much," he said. "But I have a boyfriend," she said, "and I'm in love with him."

It was as if the towel had been thrown into the boxing ring for his sake. He was out and he hadn't had a say in it. He could do just one thing: show some pride. He said, "I think we should go." On the way to her flat she tried to water down her previous words and soothe his hurt pride, but to no avail. He stopped way before they'd reached her flat and told her, "I think we shouldn't see each other anymore." She was hurt, especially after all her efforts to try to propitiate him. "OK," she said, but she couldn't find the strength to tell him anything mean; it just wasn't in her nature. Her expression showed anger for a second, but then it turned into pure disappointment. Like someone who's lost a loved one and is in denial at first, she looked at him for a second as if she were going to try to retrieve the situation, but she instantly gave up and accepted his resolution with resignation. It was his right and she understood him; she thought he was a gentle person, as she did with everyone she met. She emanated gentleness and that was why she felt everyone was kind to her.

Later on, he couldn't keep his promise to himself to never talk to her again. She went to an Italian meeting six months after the boyfriend incident and she met Elio. Manuel was good friends with the Italian guy and he didn't want to spoil his good humor, so he forced himself to be nice to Valentina. In a second meeting, he saw her eyes glare with joy when he looked at her for the first time and another glare, even more intense, when he said a few words to her. For a moment, he thought her interest in Elio was a sham whose aim was to make him feel jealous. Later on, he heard they'd met alone, so his doubts were dispersed. However, some months later he had to console his friend when he told him that Valentina had gone back to Ukraine to marry her boyfriend.

Manuel couldn't believe that girl was still in the same situation he'd left her in a year before. Her hopeless love seemed resilient to reality. He needed to ask her what it was all about to calm his unrest. As usual, she was equivocal, but she was so candid that the situation became obvious. She loved her boyfriend, but he'd left her to go and train in the U.S.; they weren't together because he didn't believe in long-distance relationships, but she knew he was on a visa and he'd have to come back, so she waited for him. He was coming back to Ukraine in a few months and they'd resumed the relationship that had been paused two years before. They talked every day and she couldn't wait to finish the semester and go back to Ukraine. She told Manuel all this face-to-face, because she was so intrigued that he'd asked her to meet again after a year. His reaction wasn't at all something she could've predicted. He didn't congratulate her, which she didn't resent, but he made no comment at all about her situation. He simply said, "That's very selfish of you." "What's selfish?" she asked, really interested in his opinion.

"You come here and try to have fun with me, then you induce my friend to believe that you're interested in him and now you just go back and fulfill your childish dream of marrying your prince charming."

"He is my prince charming, you're right, but you're wrong about all the rest. I didn't induce Elio to believe anything. I was just dazzled by him and he's so courteous. I didn't want to hurt his feelings, but I can't help feeling what I feel; my life is in Ukraine and my heart too. And as for you, I like you Manuel, and were it not for my boyfriend, I would've been with you."

"So behave as if you don't have one. Pretend you've been born again and stay."

"I can't, Manuel. My heart is too old to support a new birth. I must go back to where I belong."

"Vale, you'll always be one of the things that didn't happen to me that I regret the most."

"And you'll always be a nice memory."

" I hate that. I'd prefer to be a nightmare that haunts you, but you're too good for that. Anyway, I wish you all the best with your future husband."

"Thanks. Goodbye, Manuel."

Chapter sixteen: Manuel and Marina

Marina had deleted Manuel from Facebook a couple of times, just to add him again when she forgave him. The longest period of silence between them took place after a moment of hesitation on his part. He'd met a new girl that awoke romantic feelings in him, the same kind of feelings he'd had for Marina. Then a war started in his mind and all the advances this new girl made were repelled by memories of Marina. He committed the mistake of believing that telling this to Marina could solve something, but it only worsened the situation because now Marina's hopes were renewed and Manuel felt twice as much pressure as before. In the end, he broke up with the girl he was going out with and went to see Marina, who had moved to another city. She assumed that he'd broken up for her and had her hopes up. Manuel wanted to see Marina; he also hoped that the sight of her would rekindle his old passion for her, but that wasn't the case. There were no fresh feelings of attraction, just the nostalgia of a relationship with a nice person. He liked her personality and her romanticism, but he didn't find her attractive. However, this feeling wasn't clear to him at the moment so he wasn't clear with her either. She kissed him and he kissed her back, but nothing more happened. He went back home and wrote to her, after analyzing his feelings, that he wasn't attracted to her. She got upset and deleted him from Facebook and didn't talk to him or answer his messages for three months.

Manuel continued to send sporadic messages to her, because she always read them, even though she didn't answer them. One day, she added him back and resumed their friendship where it had been left off. He was happy to talk with her again and he was happy that she'd gotten over him. He was single at that time and he appreciated the fact of being able to count on someone whenever he felt lonely. She was also fun and he liked to know all the important details of her life, so they talked almost every day. When she first mentioned Szymon, it had already been three months since she'd met him. Manuel was very happy for her and he tried to encourage that relationship without hurting her pride by being too enthusiastic about it. So he adopted a playful jealous tone whenever she mentioned Szymon. She was simply delighted, which made her mentioned him very often. Szymon became part of the culture between Manuel and

her, which helped her assimilate him into her life. By the time she'd
analyzed her feelings, Szymon was as indispensable to her as
Manuel and she would've had trouble if either of them had asked her
to not see the other anymore. But this didn't happen. For Manuel,
there was no reason to do that and neither was there for Szymon,
because he didn't even know about Manuel's existence.
Marina's feelings were airtight. She'd cry sometimes, but if Szymon
saw her, she'd never mention Manuel as one of her sorrows. She
could always come up with a more current excuse. She didn't need
Szymon to know about her feelings; she just needed his soothing
presence and his comforting arms. Once she learned to value
Manuel's brotherly love without expecting anything more, she
became so happy to have two people who really cared about her. She
wasn't alone anymore and the world became much less hostile to her.

Chapter seventeen: Elio
After his divorce from Valentina, Elio was simply emotionally
ruined. He was already fifty-five years old and he didn't have a care
in the world, which was negative at his age. His daughter had moved
to another country, so there was nothing that tied him to Italy
anymore. They'd moved there for economic reasons after he'd
married Valentina, and now he was left alone in a country that didn't
offer him much emotional relief. He decided to go back to Poland to
try to meet a young Polish girl who could revive his heart. He
contacted his old friend Manuel, who was very glad about the news
and offered him a place to stay till he could find somewhere to live.
As soon as he arrived in Poland, he boosted the Italian meetings with
his presence and met a lot of young girls who wanted to improve
their language skills. He was a sociable person, and he enjoyed the
company of beautiful girls, but his loneliness wasn't appeased by
visual pleasure. He wanted to find some sense of belonging, so he
asked women to speak Polish to him. Some of them were amused for

a while, listening to him blabber in Polish, and others were simply annoyed, but there were some whose maternal instinct kicked in and who talked to him as if they were talking to a child of theirs. Among these women was Marta, a forty-year-old blonde whose life had left her with neither a husband nor a child to care about. She spoke broken Italian, so she didn't mind Elio's broken Polish. She found him handsome, even though he was fifteen years older. She didn't have any vanity left when it came to relationships; she'd been alone for a long time and she wasn't looking for a sire to fecundate her and take care of her kids, but she was looking for good company in the declining years of her life. Elio didn't feel the same way, though; he desired a fertile female that could provoke a storm of fecundation in him and Marta wasn't particularly fit for the role. However, she kept him company in his loneliest periods, when he had to deal with everyday issues such as feeding himself and killing time till sleep came. She became his stronghold and his underrated lover, but she never complained about it.

When Manuel listened to him talk about Marta, he didn't know what to make of it. He felt his friend had at last found his place, but that he wasn't aware of it yet. He understood the situation: Elio had been looking for himself for so long that now that he'd found himself, he couldn't assimilate it. Elio wasn't totally satisfied with Marta, but he was totally dissatisfied with his life, so it was just understandable that he would complain about her too. Manuel hoped his friend would get over his frustration soon and learn what he really wanted: whether he wanted Marta in his life or not. Little did he know that Elio would never make that decision and that he'd always complain about Marta's age, without ever thinking seriously about leaving her. The years passed in that way and Marta's proverbial lack of attractiveness became part of their common culture and source of humor. Manuel would often say "How's the beauty doing?" whenever he wanted to know about her and Elio would sometimes answer with this formula: "I don't know, but the beast is sleeping at home."

Chapter Eighteen: Manuel

Marina had recently married Szymon and Manuel had gone to their wedding. It was the first Polish wedding he'd been to and he had only one concern during the whole night: To turn down the shots of vodka in the most polite way possible. He succeeded in ending the night in a relatively proper state; at least he remembered which country he was in, because he heard Polish all around him, and how many months there were till the next World Cup, because someone had mentioned that Argentina was definitively going to win this time. The rest was blurry: his reason for being in that country, his reason for staying that long, his failure to fulfill his most important goal in Poland: to settle down.

When he was a young man, he would've never thought that he'd become more infantile the more he aged, but that's what actually happened to him. After a period of maturity in which his ambitions and unfulfilled desires had made him absorb a little pragmatism from the world, he was back to his eternal idealism. Now that physiology was under the control of his mind, he started recycling his accumulated idealistic feelings and thoughts. There was one idea that obsessed him more than anything else at that moment, and it was as arbitrary as his phone number. He had a nostalgic feeling for Argentina and it was all channeled into love for songs in Spanish. He'd seldom listen to songs in any other language when he was looking for an outlet for his emotions. He just couldn't cry in English or Polish and he found it pretentious in Polish people that they posted a song in English on Facebook to convey their current mood. "Let them cry in English then, but my feelings are Spanish," he'd think at those moments.

This loyalty to his own language drove him to an expansive feeling of pride for songs in Spanish; he'd always find a suitable song to play to a girl he'd just met. Many girls just answered that it sounded nice, but they didn't understand anything, which was a positive comment. Some girls upheld the Polish tradition of uncalled-for honesty and they said, "It's OK, but not my favorite kind of music." He went on playing songs to girls just to get disappointed in a Little Prince fashion, until he met Ela. Now Ela wasn't into romantic stuff, but she was into Manuel, which made up for every fault of hers. She saw Manuel's irremediable idealism and she knew how to handle it. She'd never completely contradict him, but she would create an opinion on the issues that interested him because she knew she'd lose his respect if she didn't. She was malleable as clay and she didn't mind being indoctrinated into his worldview; she didn't see any danger in his extreme ideas, the same as she didn't worry about their ill consequences. She could feel which of his ideas were to be kept only in the realm of theory and which ones could be put into practice. She knew when to take him seriously and when to overlook his words.

So when he sent her the first song, one of his favorite boleros, she instinctively knew what she had to do. She lied with all her heart. She lied as if her life depended on it. She didn't tell a white lie that was meant to get out of an awkward situation. Her lie was Machiavellianly confected so he'd never realize it wasn't true. She didn't go into commonplaces nor was she flattering or vague. She nailed an answer that only the most fanatical lover of boleros could've uttered; she said, "Nice song," and she hummed the chorus. That was all it took to make him believe that the song had touched her emotionally and that they shared a common passion.

Once she knew she'd gained his favor, she added a dose of humor to her comment: "That song makes me cry."

"Why does it make you cry?" he asked.

"Because I see the passion and I don't understand it," she said.

"It's very simple," he said, and he explained the song to her.

"I love it," she said.

"It's nothing special," he said, to be honest with her. He'd sent her the song because something she'd said had reminded him of it, but he didn't think there was anything special about it.

"For me it's special," she said.

"Why?'" he asked.

"Because you explained it so well." She smiled.

Now he thought of sending her a better song to educate her taste in boleros, but he knew it wouldn't have the same effect as that song, because it had been the first one. He regretted not having planned the whole thing better, but then he thought that life is always like that. We don't appreciate the intrinsic value of things but rather their value with respect to ourselves. Songs become ingrained in our brains if we listen to them on special occasions and their value increases as we cherish those memories.

Chapter Nineteen: Manuel and Ela

Just to add drama to their love story, Ela never told Manuel that she was into him and, to compound his anguish, she had a boyfriend. She told him just after they met, because she was going to meet him at a party in the city he lived in.

"I'm going there to meet my future fiance," she said at first. And he summoned up the courage to make sure she wasn't joking or she hadn't made a typo while writing during the chat.

"Are you engaged?" he asked

"No!" she wrote, "I'm too young to be engaged."

Then he thought she was simply joking about meeting the man of her life at that party, so he said,

"But first you need to have a boyfriend if you want a fiance."

"I don't need a boyfriend. I'm a modern woman," she said, "but I love him and I'll marry him one day. But not now, in around ten years."

He was confused and exasperated. Was she joking again? He didn't know what to say to force a serious answer from her.

"What's his name?" he asked to try to bring the conversation into the realm of reality.

"Franek," she said, "and he's gonna be a good father for my kids. He's a religious person."

Now he felt he was dealt a double blow. She certainly had a boyfriend and she wanted a religious guy. The feeling of a gap widening between them was overwhelming. But he wouldn't allow his silence to betray his heart, so he went on writing:

"So we can say he's your boyfriend then."

"I prefer 'future fiance'," she said.

"Well," he said, "in Spanish you would actually call your boyfriend your fiance. We don't have a word for it. We just have *novio* and *novia*, which literally mean fiance, but which may also mean just boyfriend or girlfriend."

"Haha," she wrote, in a perfect imitation of what may well have been authentic laughter. Manuel felt like writing a book entitled: *Girls with boyfriends. How to deal with them.* He'd already had some experience and all he could advise to guys in the same situation was to get the hell out of it as fast as possible. But, like any good philosopher, he wouldn't follow his own advice. He was the one meant to be sacrificed for the sake of knowledge. He'd learn everything that needed to be learned to warn future generations about the evils lurking in the shadows of a jealous heart. He knew it would be easier to forget about her, to go on seeking girls who were pretty and available, but his worldly experience also told him that it would be difficult to find such a beautiful girl again. He'd probably see many in the streets or on random trams and at tram stops, but he wouldn't connect with them as he'd done with this girl. And she was so objectively beautiful that it felt wrong to dismiss the smallest chance he could have of being with her. And he saw that chance at that moment. His heart wrapped the information his mind processed in romantic hopes. The fact of her telling him she had a future fiance took the form of a disclosure of an intimate desire for a fiance, which she didn't have yet. He knew that women, the same as God, work in mysterious ways, so he left the information she'd given him open to new interpretations.

Chapter Twenty: Valentina
The honeymoon was glorious. She'd married her prince charming, the one she'd washed herself in tears for. He took her to dream land, with a stopover in Amsterdam. They arrived at Atlanta's airport in less time than it would've taken her to lower her excitement enough to sleep. It wasn't so much the country, it could've been anywhere in the world; it was the adventure, the thrill of incertitude that this beginning of the rest of her life gave her. For theirs was not meant to be an ordinary marriage, foreboded by a boring domestic honeymoon; theirs was the world to conquer and the youthful illusion that a responsible life can also be fun. And they lived out their illusion, but they couldn't outlive it. Their prospects for the future, as well as all their enthusiasm, were undermined on that journey.
The thing is, that journey represented the climax of their relationship, and once it was over, they just saw the dreary life in front of them. For although Valentina knew she wanted to be a mother, she wasn't the kind of girl who gets pregnant by accident. Nor was she a woman that would engender a conscious being just for the sake of a marriage. And that was actually her mistake: she confused the goal of having a child with the reason for getting married. Because she had the fancy idea that a child should crown the perfect union among two people, and it shouldn't be precipitated. So she'd married the guy who rocked her world, but she hadn't quite

thought it over. She hadn't realized that, out of the five years she'd been in love with him, they'd only been officially together for three, and had only been living in the same country for one-year-and-a-half. She enjoyed the unachievable dream he represented for her, but now their relationship was too stable to provoke any exhilaration in her. She'd married because she was a conservative girl, but she was also a modern girl who wouldn't accept less than full happiness in her life. He didn't push it either; he was too busy fleeing from the doom of a Ukrainian life. He also wanted kids in his life, but they would never be a priority. He had too many things to catch up with: wealth and things he'd been denied from childhood; it was his Ukranian karma.

Thus, they became a modern married couple: barren and self-serving. Although they diplomatically interacted with other couples and they maintained a civil attitude towards people they happened to meet, their only reason for their socializing was to strengthen their relationship. Every philanthropic act was done just to show the world how valuable they were as a couple, just to unconsciously make up for the purposelessness of their relationship. The truth is, they could've been as happy single, living together in a looser relationship than marriage, or they could've turned totally modern and treated marriage as a legal contract done for simple practical reasons. But they were already married and it was a heavy burden on them. So they did what a modern couple with traditional values does: they were dishonest with themselves. She started treating him with increasing coldness and he started to dissociate his emotional from his physical feelings. They wouldn't have sex for weeks just because she didn't see any point in it, and he would start responding to other women's smiles. And as they were a modern couple, things evolved quite naturally. He was technically doing nothing wrong, just socializing with women, and one smile led to another, until he found himself in front of an appetizing body, with inviting eyes and a tacitly encouraging mouth. And just at the moment he understood what was going on, he knew that instincts were more powerful than mores and that he'd been a victim of a social illusion. And for that reason, he didn't feel so guilty when Valentina learned about his affair four months later. He actually praised himself for trying to save their marriage, even though it wasn't giving him any satisfaction. For him, they were more than even, and now it was up to Valentina to decide what to make of their current situation. Valentina felt outraged, hurt and demoralized by the news. But for the first time in a long time she felt herself again. She did the only thing to be done and she felt whole at last. She kicked him out of their house and agreed to an equal distribution of property so she wouldn't have to talk to him again. Her relatives consoled her by telling her that she'd married too young and that she was still young enough to marry again, so she shouldn't worry about that. For Valentina, it was the end of a fantasy and the beginning of her real life, besieged by the banalities of being single, like loneliness, empty hours of leisure and more freedom than a human being can handle sometimes. She missed the stability of marriage, the constrained life in which she'd felt so confident. Now she spent the same amount of time and mental effort trying to make decisions alone as she had with her husband and, at the end of the day, she felt less fulfilled. She was like an animal raised in captivity, which now that it is free doesn't know how to behave in the wild. She'd been domesticated and now the only thing for her to do was to find a new master.

Chapter Twenty-One: Marina and Valentina
From the moment she saw her, she hated her guts. She'd seen a seductive blond girl in front of the love of her life and she couldn't take it. She found every excuse to hate her, even though Valentina was quite nice to her, as she was to everyone she spoke to. But Marina wouldn't take any crap from her; she didn't want that walking

temptation to be around Manuel. That's why, when she heard that Valentina was going out with Elio, she was beside herself with joy at the beginning, but apprehensive later on. She still remembered the muscle flexing between her and Valentina over Manuel, and how difficult it had been for her to finally mark her territory and keep that bitch outside the proper boundaries. Valentina had never seemed to put up a fight, but Marina knew very well about a woman's ways and she wouldn't celebrate victory until she'd seen the defeated corpse of her enemy. And she couldn't be careful enough to check whether going out with Elio wasn't just a strategy of Valentina's to make Manuel jealous. But finally Marina could relax when Valentina broke up with Elio to go back to Ukraine and marry her boyfriend back there.

Now they met again after two years. Valentina had told Marina that she was coming back to Poland to try to fix her life. Marina felt for her and wanted to help, but she didn't see how she could. She listened to the story of her marriage to the Ukrainian guy and she twinged with compassion at every word, but when the delicate topic came up, Marina was at a loss what to say. Valentina had just asked her how Manuel was doing and whether they were still together. Marina answered her that they'd broken up more than a year before and Manuel had already been seeing another girl for four months. She saw the deception in Valentina's eyes and she finally understood it all, the reason why Valentina had come back to Poland and the strange fact that she'd contacted her of all people. She couldn't help feeling annoyed but also sorry at Valentina's utilitarianism. She felt used, but not as a servant is used by their master; rather as a doctor is used by their patient. She felt proud of herself, of the course her life had taken, away from Manuel and into a new beginning, and she felt the more sorry about Valentina's situation.

After the bomb was dropped, Valentina didn't show much interest in conversing any longer. Marina gave in to the general mood of the meeting and her conversation waned. That was the last time they talked to each other.

Valentina and Elio

Of course, Valentina confirmed with her own eyes what she'd heard from Marina. Of course she tried not to believe it at first, but she ended up accepting it. She still remembered the day when she was leaving for Ukraine to marry her boyfriend. There was a clear blue sky in Warsaw that day and she'd gone for a walk with Manuel. It was so unusual for them to meet alone again, but fate had wanted it that way. Manuel was supposed to come to visit Elio, who was devastated by the situation, but he made an intentional mistake and went to visit Valentina instead. Valentina was gladly surprised by the visit and asked Manuel in, but he looked like a trapped animal, so she proposed going for a walk. He agreed listlessly, but it was evident that something way more important than his location was on his mind. Finally, when they were sitting on a bench in their favorite park, he told her that she couldn't leave without breaking his heart and that she was probably the love of his life. She listened to his declaration carefully and weighted it against all her plans to marry the love of her youth back in Ukraine and be happy ever after, and she gave her verdict. "I'm sorry Manuel, I like you very much, but I love him." The word "love" seemed to have a stronger resonance than "being really attracted to someone" to her, even though she didn't know what that word meant. For she had thus named her feelings for her Ukrainian boyfriend, a mix of habit and common memories, with a pinch of melancholy and drama. She knew the ropes of relationships already, but she didn't know their essence: simple but never waxing attraction.

It was this attraction that had brought her back to Poland, and she wasn't going to surrender without a fight. She called him to ask how he was doing and, after not hearing any invitation to meet up, she asked him to come to her hostel, that evening if possible. He appeared at her door the next afternoon, just after finishing work, and she received him with such composure that no one would've guessed what was going on inside her. She led the conversation towards his relationship with his new girlfriend and asked, in the end, if he felt for that girl the same as he'd felt for her. Manuel said he did, and that Ela was everything he wished for. During the whole conversation, she tried to find a fissure in his apparently solid relationship with his new girlfriend, but she found none. She asked him, as her last resort, if he still felt something for her, to which Manuel answered with a simple but efficient: "No, I have new feelings now."

She was too despondent to gather enough strength to go back to Ukraine. She stayed at a cheap hostel and couldn't even have enough confidence in the future to look for an apartment. She was in a lethargic state when she heard someone knock at her room door. She opened it to see Elio, staring warmly at her. How could she resist such a manifestation of love? She hugged him and sought his lips. He kissed her passionately.

Three months later, as if trying to catch up in the race in which she'd lagged behind, she married him. Of course, she invited Manuel and Marina, who tried to hide her astonishment in order to show her happiness for Valentina. Of course, Valentina tried to be happy with Elio, of course. But Elio had also deceived himself. He'd thought that the forbidden fruit was what was missing in his life, while it was actually simple bread he was yearning for. And the bread didn't come but only sporadic feasts of that delicacy that he'd gotten so used to and that he dared call: Valentina's love. Twenty years and a daughter later, when he saw that his hunger was never going to be satiated with her, he asked Valentina for a divorce. Then, when his daughter was so busy that she barely had time to visit her old father, he cried alone in his flat in Warsaw while missing his beloved Italy.

What became of Valentina, we already know. Or rather we don't know, as we don't know with precision what became of Manuel, Marina and Elio. They're still alive, all of them, and they're still trying to be happy, some of them more successfully than others.

A dream and its interpretation

I can never remember my dreams. It's one of my biggest regrets. They are so vivid and so imaginative that, were I able to recall them at will, I'm sure I'd be a better writer. When I was a kid, I used to be able to remember my dreams more frequently and vividly than now. No, it seems that my consciousness dismisses them as futile as soon as it takes over. So I have no more access to my subconscious other than a glimpse of it sometimes when I'm waking up. And, sadly enough, it's a well of images and emotions.

But this time I managed to remember the idea of my dream. I was at my grandmother's; that's the only detail I remember. It must have been an important detail since I remember it. Generally, when we wake up, we retain the last picture of the dream, that is, the last moment we lived before waking up, the moment when our subconscious life was cut short. The strange thing is that, from there, dreams start to vanish not in chronological order but in order of relevance; that is, we end up remembering only the essence of a dream, if we remember anything at all.

So I have this picture of the dream I lived through last night. It's not a horror dream in the technical sense, but it was horrific in the real sense. Terror may be awoken by dangerous situations, but it's generally more insidious when it has to do with hidden fears. And that's what scares me the most about this dream in particular: that it doesn't look like a horror dream at all, but is it?

Now I must confess I didn't make any strenuous effort to try to preserve the dream because I immediately started thinking about reality when I woke up. I was in bed with a girl I'm not in love with and her presence distracted me from my dream. I talked to her and started caressing her to wake myself up because I needed to go to work. Arousal proves to be an effective stimulant. So I left aside the inquiry about the meaning of the dream I'd just had. But as soon as we departed and I started driving to work, I started thinking of the most plausible interpretation for my dream.

Now the most clear interpretation for me is that, since I'm not in love with my girlfriend, I have remorseful feelings about being halfheartedly with her and fears about the karmic consequences of breaking up with her in the future.

So now the dream. I was at my grandmother's house lying in bed with someone. I don't remember what we were doing, but it must have been something incriminating. I deduce this from the guilty feeling I got afterwards, when my girlfriend arrived. Up to now the dream is very clear, almost trivial, I would say, and I would add that I expected much more from the mind of a writer. But here's where the artistic trait kicks in, I guess, because there's a small detail that changes the whole possible interpretation of the dream. This detail consists of the fact that the person who was lying in bed with me was a man. Now, as I said, I don't remember exactly what we were doing, but I remember the overpowering fear of being discovered when I heard my girlfriend entering my grandmother's house, so my only guess is that, to my great distress, we were doing something sexual. Now, I can't imagine why I was just distressed about it just when my girlfriend came, and not before, since the conscious idea of touching another man is simply horrific to me. I therefore surmised that I must have been lying in bed with a girl who then became a man when my girlfriend arrived. That would be the easiest answer, but to be honest there was no feeling of surprise about the man in my bed but rather a pervasive feeling of guilt.

Now, you can imagine the horror a heterosexual male born and raised in a patriarchal society may feel when he realizes he's had a homosexual dream, and if you can't, let me illustrate it for you. Imagine you're in the kitchen eating something with great delight. Now your mother enters and she's ordered you not to eat anything before meals, so you're startled and full of remorse at having disobeyed her. Then you happen to look down and there, in the dish, lies the food you were filling your mouth with with so much pleasure. As it happens, it's shit. I mean feces, poo, excrement. I can't really emphasize enough the alarm a normal person would feel, but you feel nothing but guilt at having eating between meals; nothing more, not even wonder at eating something that people don't even like looking at. Now, if you didn't get upset when you dreamed about eating crap, I'd say you're abnormal. So I feel the same about myself now. Mind you, I know that half of the human population eat crap, metaphorically speaking if we follow the analogy, since half of the population are women and they hunger for men. But that's not a relief since I'm not supposed to be eating crap but to delight in delicious food. The only moment I could feel that eating crap is remotely similar to eating delicious food is when I have indigestion; therefore, this is the best interpretation for my dream: I'm metaphorically eating something without hunger so I get indigestion from it; then my subconscious, with the dark humor that characterizes it, told me that I might as well have been eating shit. Now the last detail, my grandmother's house. That's not so strange because it was the place where I used to play around with my older cousin when I was a small kid. I hadn't had an erection yet so the only thing I wanted to do to her was to kiss her on the mouth, but she was in full puberty so she made me kiss her on other parts of her body. The general feeling of that experience is one of deceived innocence. I think this detail in my dream means that I realized something I was unaware of, the same as later on in life I realized the meaning of what I'd done with my cousin. This detail of the dream is the most disturbing one because it may be just one thing: I'm afraid one day I'll realize something I've been missing during all this time.

Three days to heaven

He was certain he would survive this time. He had died so many times before, but this time it just felt different. Probably because he didn't want it anymore; he wanted to live eternally as written in some book he'd read. He didn't want that state of non-existence anymore. There was no memory of those moments, those breaks in the continuum of life. But he remembered everything else. The mechanism by which our brains forget everything that is currently not in use did not function for him. He could remember every single detail of past existences and he was simply tired of repeating himself. There was practically nothing he could do that would've been a novelty; he'd tried being good, bad, wise and stupid. He'd tried strict honesty and blatant shamelessness and now there was nothing else to try. He would also consider the option of stopping existing, as he'd read in some other book; to stop the madness of being born and inventing a goal for his current life cycle.

At least if he didn't die this time he could spare himself the annoyance of childhood and adolescence. There was nothing new for him to learn from that phase; he'd been born in thirty different places and learned more than fifty languages during his different lives. He had realized that the purpose of successful communication was rather in excluding people from linguistic interaction than in creating a common means by which people could express their thoughts. He'd seen dialects evolve into indistinguishable languages for the sake of national identity. He'd been inculcated in a great variety of customs that were supposed to help him fit into the society he had been born into. But he'd seldom made use of the social rules learned. He'd realized that conventions were made to be broken by people who were supposed to be above social rules. And he always managed to put himself above the law of Man and its intricacies.

But he didn't like the aches of old age either, so he would try something to break out of the perpetual life cycle. He was thirty-three and, from experience, he knew that was the best age to become immortal. The body was fully developed and slightly aged, but the brain, the most important body part, was at its apex. Being immortal also implied recovering full functionality of every organ, so it didn't matter if he'd injured himself before or if he'd worn down an organ too much; everything would be restored to its optimal state. But how to become immortal? That question had haunted him for several lives now, and he'd tried to leap into immortality many times before, just to find himself covered in amniotic fluid once again. But he was positive he would survive this time. It had been predicted in another book. He knew it because he'd written the books himself.

In this book, he'd written about the way in which he'd be killed and the reason why. He would pronounce his immortality in public until religious leaders felt threatened by him. To do that, he would perform apparently supernatural acts, like making souls come back from inaction. He knew that all souls go into a lethargic state once their karmic cycle has finished a revolution, so he managed to deceive souls into momentary wakefulness by disrupting their karmic cycle. He'd announced that he was going to resurrect people. People who were mourning the dead had heard about his powers, which had been predicted by the manuscripts he himself had written, so they couldn't accept the deaths of their loved ones when they saw him; they expected them to be alive again. So they were. In such a way, he also healed people who had been injured or were handicapped. He altered their karma by promising them complete redemption from it, which they believed in. This belief was strong enough to free them from their karmic load for a lifetime, and thus they were healed. To further convince people, he also did some magic tricks, including levitating, substance transmutation and sleight of hand materialization of objects. He'd honed these skills for several lives and he was the best magician that ever existed, so even magicians from that time were deceived by his magic.

But the real miracle he wanted to perform was not to die this time. To do that, he needed to fulfill what he'd laid down in that manuscript. This manuscript had been read by many, who were expecting everything to be fulfilled. But he could not get people to believe that the place and time of the prediction were right, so several times he'd died in vain. Obviously, he could not choose where he was born, so he had had to resort to smart maneuvers to make people believe he'd been actually born where predicted. But this time he actually had been born where predicted, which had amazed him at first, but now seemed totally normal to him. He believed his karma was bringing him closer to his desired goal. Also, people took him seriously this time. He'd managed to scare many people and gather many followers. He just needed to die an outstanding death, which could remain in the collective memory for long enough to outweigh the expectation of new life after death that is natural to men. His death had to be so horrendous that it would be revived again and again in people's minds. Only in that way he could be immortal. Because from the moment people forgot about his death, his karmic cycle would reach a full revolution and he'd be reborn.

Thus it happened. And he was never born again, but he went back to his body after three days. His followers did as they were commanded and they helped him out of the grave where his corpse had been laid. Now he wanders freely among mortals, and his wisdom is ever greater. Passions and instincts are appeased in him; he just lives for knowledge. He cannot die or be killed, because the collective mind brings him back to his eternal death and therefore his eternal body although nobody really knows what this body looks like.

Love and innocence

If I hadn't met disillusion in your eyes,
if I hadn't been abandoned in my hopes,
if I hadn't lost my mind for you,
if I could always sleep at night,
I wouldn't be writing a new story,
and I wouldn't be alive.

Every real love story starts in innocence; that's how it always should be. Then this innocence is tested, but it always prevails; otherwise, it wouldn't be real love. Love that gives way to passion and basic instincts is not real love and does not deserve literary endorsement. Because in the literary world we can allow ourselves to be idealistic and to praise that which we can seldom achieve in real life. And, nevertheless, if we lowered the standard of our ideals, what would become of our realities?

Once there was a girl, whose name was Innocence. And there also was a young man, whose name was Love. Innocence was an attentive, obedient and tender daughter, whose candidness was the joy of her parents. She was righteous and honest, and very considerate when making decisions. She was selfless in her goals; the most important thing in the world for her was not to disappoint her parents' faith in her.

Love was a dreamer. He idealized women to the point of not daring to talk to the object of his desire. He only got what might be called his first girlfriend at the age of twenty. Because he was so shy, he had not been able to straightforwardly approach the girls he was in love with before. He didn't know how to deal with sex; it was something that he desired, but which he found incompatible with his idealistic views on women. His romantic fantasies always ended in front of the bedroom door, and any thought that trespassed across that threshold was considered pornographic, foul, contemptible. He dissociated these thoughts from the objects of his adoration, lest they become impure.

When Innocence met the first man she fell in love with, she barely foresaw the revolution that was taking place inside her. She had never been selfish, so she had never thought of the possibility of falling in love before. Whenever she did something, she did it dutifully rather than passionately, so she didn't know how to react to the feelings that were stirring in her. She tried to rationalize the situation by creating duties towards the young man that had conquered her heart. The smallest gesture of kindness from him was an excuse for her dutiful adoration. In the end, when all the barriers of her modesty were overcome, there was nothing that she could not do for him. She moderated his passion and tried to guide him towards righteous feelings, but she would not deny him the fulfillment of his wishes.

Love's first breakup had cut him deeply. He was studying philosophy at that time and he found no more sense in his studies. Life lost all meaning for him and he quit what he was doing and decided to dedicate himself to the only source of consolation he had left: music. He tried to rediscover a sense of harmony with life, which he had evidently lost. After almost two years of full days playing music, he recovered his sanity and could come back to reality again. He decided to start studying again, but this time something more productive: law. At university he met a beautiful girl, who happened to be interested in him. They had a couple of dates and, after a couple of months, she finally admitted her feelings towards him. He thought of marriage and kids with her, of a big house and lazy Sundays, where his only concern was to make her happy.

It was gradual. No one can say that it was because of her economic circumstances, because Innocence never lacked anything at home.

However, when she moved in with her boyfriend, everything changed for her. She felt useless and she was too young and inexperienced to be able to get a proper job. She tried odd jobs, which were compatible with her studies, but her boyfriend's demands added an extra load that she could not bear. She took care of the household chores and let him take care of the money for rent and food, as he was older than her and better positioned in the professional market. But he started making implicit remarks that he resented the fact that she didn't bring money into their home, and she was disheartened. The diminution of her self-love was gradual, but by the end of a process of psychological manipulation and emotional extortion, she found herself helpless and ready to transgress every moral law she knew to make him happy. That is why, one day, when he came home accompanied by another young man and told her that this person would be sharing the bed with her for thirty minutes, she froze with horror and died inside, but she didn't refuse. She did as ordered and entered the bedroom with the man the love of her life had brought home. This situation was repeated numerous times, and although she knew she'd lost the love of her life's respect, she knew he was satisfied with her financial contribution to their home. When she left him, Love was devastated. She alleged that she'd never pronounced the magic words, as if saying "I love you" was a sort of legal liability which, if not pronounced, makes you exempt from any responsibility. That's why she left without any remorse when she found a role that better suited her beauty and expectations. Love had overcome various disappointments and he believed he was strong enough to overcome this one too, but he wasn't aware of a great weakness in his character. His instinct kicked in as soon as she left; his seed looked for urgent fertile ground where it would be saved from annihilation. He didn't pay attention to the signs of his body, and he dulled himself with alcohol to avoid hearing this inner voice that prompted him to action. Until one night on which, to his disconcertion, he found himself semi-drunk and in front of a brothel. There were girls of all sizes and colors inside, like flowers ready to be plucked. He picked the one he fancied the most, unconsciously choosing the one that looked the purest, and he entered a private room with her. He repeated this action several times, picking different flowers each time, and in that way he managed to momentarily quieten the call of the wild resonating inside him. Innocence broke up with the man whom she'd unconditionally loved. She still loved him, so she didn't wish him any bad. He tried to coerce her to keep working for him, but she decided to set up on her own. There was nothing else she knew how to do and she was used to a life of expenditure. She was pleased with her comfortable, free life, until she met Love.

Love was looking at ads, as usual, selectively clicking on only the options that were worth the effort, when he happened to rest his eyes on Innocence. Her face was covered, as is usual in these ads, and her price was not too high. He called. He got an immediate appointment and he went, excited to have a new dose of ephemeral intimacy. Innocence opened the door and he could not resist it, it had always been his flaw, he fell in love with a total stranger. Of course, he felt that it would pass soon. How many times had he felt something similar after seeing a beautiful girl at a tram stop or on a bus? Their non-reaction, their lack of reciprocation had neutralized his emerging feelings and he'd lived normally ever after. But this time it was different; she was different. She was doing her job, but she was not deprived of feelings. At the beginning, she felt a strong preference towards him and she wished all her clients were like him. But when he was leaving, she wished he was her only client for ever after.

He didn't search for new ads anymore; he came back to her every time. He was jealous, of course, but the situation wasn't any different from that of a young man in love with a girl with a boyfriend. He knew she slept with someone else, and that ate at him, but he did the same, or at least he tried. However, he couldn't restrain himself any longer and he grabbed her, while she was getting off him, and forced her to lie at his side. She wasn't startled, but she stared at him expectantly. He told her that he could not bear the idea of her sleeping with other men and that she should please stop that or she'd drive him crazy. She didn't expect such a petition and she didn't know what to say so she said nothing. She lay with him and he didn't budge either. When her phone rang, she didn't answer. She nestled her head on his chest and closed her eyes. They slept. When they woke up it was morning already. A new day had dawned and they didn't want to think of the previous night. And they never did. They built their new life from that day on, and nothing else mattered anymore.

On love and other demons

Romantic love does not exist, because love and romance exclude each other. Romance is self- centered and seeks freedom while love is selfless and seeks responsibility. Love is not loud and spontaneous like romance, but quiet and steady. Our aim in life should be to think romantically, but to love realistically. Because love is a concept that has been misused so much that it has gained a mysticism which makes it seem hard to define. That is why, to define love, we need to take the time to define what love is not: romance. But that leads to a very subtle error that is generally made: To think that love is the desirable evolution of romance, or that love is superior than romance.

As I said before, love and romance exclude each other. So, following this logic, there is no hierarchical connection between them. But why do we confuse them? Because they can actually coexist. Now this does not make sense at all, but let's try to elucidate. If they are obviously opposite to each other, how is it possible that they exist together? Because that is our human nature. There is love and hate in us, and both are positive forces that help us develop. Love is the acceptance of our circumstances and the steady work needed to fulfill our responsibilities. Hate is rebellion and trying to find new ways of seeing our realities. The task of philosophers is mainly one of hatred. They don't accept reality but want to change it. The writer's task, when it comes to merely describing reality, is one of love, but rarely do writers confine themselves to merely describing reality. Now romance is hatred, it's pure rebellion. It doesn't care about tomorrow but about now, while love is always done with foresight. But love is so simple that it can be defined in four words: Taking care of someone.

Love is, however, almost never found by itself. Because – like the selfish beings that we are – we cannot help but love with romance, that is with hatred. A mother that loves her children is also attached to them and unconsciously inculcates them with all her fears and vices. But love is always simple: She takes care of them. However, besides loving them, she also has romantic feelings for them. Now, having feelings is obviously not wrong; the point is what we do with them. From all we have said, we must conclude that love is not natural but needs to be learned. The instinct of attachment, however, is natural, and many confuse it with love. Many say "I love you" when they mean "I want you nearby." Now, my main concern here is to correct the general mistake people make of hierarchizing love. Many believe that there are many kinds of love and that there is a special kind of love they need to reserve for a partner, a good friend, etc. We sometimes confuse love with feelings. Love is selfless so it does not depend on feelings. We should try to love every single person we meet and everything around us. Remember that to love means simply to take care of someone. There is no attachment implied, so we could legitimately say to a total stranger "I love you" while we are helping them, because we are actually loving them at that moment. Thus, a doctor attending his patients is giving them love, and also a teacher teaching her students.

Love is therefore unuttered action. It could be explicitly uttered, but this would just be prizing ourselves. To say "I love you" is simply like saying "I am generous and caring." Once we exorcise love from its demons, we can learn to love more freely, without the constraints of hierarchy and categorizations. Love is for everyone and it's something we need to do. For example, I took time to write these thoughts that may help others love more freely, and I did it out of need because I don't feel fulfilled unless I write something once in a while. People also have the need to talk to others and ask them how they are or to diligently perform their work so they can be useful to others. Love is everywhere, so we don't need to go far to look for it, and that is something we should always keep in mind.

Tejerina´s horror

Recently someone remarked that my horror stories are too violent and therefore unpleasant. I answered that I just depict the world as it is; the natural world is generous but also hostile to human kind and we need to thrive to survive. But in the urban jungle where we live, the greatest danger lurks inside ourselves and in our relations with the other inhabitants of these luxurious cages we call cities. I'm not like Stephen King, who invents horror to quench his readers' thirst for fear. I just happen to be sensitive to man-made suffering and I feel the need to tell everyone about the dangers hidden in a soul that lacks awareness. Tejerina's case reverberated throughout the whole of Argentina a long time ago, but its echo still remains in the innermost part of my memory. Such a case should have never existed, and the fact that it still does and it has its advocates saddens me. So here it is, the worst horror story I've ever told and which unfortunately happens to be a real one.

I won't write about the details of the case because they're irrelevant. There is one and only one thing to know to understand the horror of this story, but, for those of you who haven't heard about Tejerina before, I'll build up the tension so you realize the horror she must have suffered. I don't do this to entice my readers or to have fun at the expense of real suffering; I do it because I believe in empathy and I find simply inhuman the matter-of-fact way in which reporters talk about tragedies. We become desensitized by reading or watching these kinds of stories in which the human factor – feelings – is missing. Imagine Tolstoy's War and Peace or Dostoevsky's Crime and Punishment written in a matter-of-fact way and you'll see my point. These are not pieces of entertainment but socially committed stories that are not less serious because they depict feelings; on the contrary, they are more serious because of that. So here it is, the worst horror story I've ever written and which unfortunately happens to be a real one.

As I said, I won't tell you the details of the story because actually I don't remember them, but I'll tell you what I do remember. I remember hearing about a woman who was condemned to fourteen years in prison for the murder of her newborn. I remember her case sparking a heated debate about abortion in Argentina. I remember that the prosecutor had actually asked for a life sentence, but then allowed for mitigating factors. What these mitigating factors were, I can't remember right now, maybe because they were not so relevant to the case, but relevant enough to be "mitigating factors". The relevant factors were that she had given birth to her child – after a seven-month pregnancy – in her house. Immediately after the birth, she put the child into a box and stabbed it twenty times in the bathroom. Now, someone so inhuman as to kill an innocent creature should be punished with death, but maybe Argentinean judges are too generous. Actually, the whole penal system is generous. Tejerina was released from prison only seven years after her conviction. What a country to allow child murderers to walk freely in the streets! Actually, the fact that it was her own child should have been an aggravating factor, but maybe Argentinean judges understand the law better.

Now, this case still burns inside me because I've recently had the displeasure of hearing about Pope Francis's stand on abortion and also because the Polish government wants to restrict even more the abortion law by penalizing women who abort their babies. Every time I hear advocates of the pro-life movement, I clench my teeth and wish that I'll see the day when there won't be any more Tejerinas. But there still may be, maybe not so murderous, but as dehumanized as that poor woman was. What leads someone to kill their child, to abandon or abuse it? How can we force a woman to love the fruit of her womb? Isn't the pro-life way a more hideous crime than murder? Because if you kill someone, they suffer only once; you're actually harming more their loved ones by depriving them of the person's presence. But if you force a woman to undergo an unwanted pregnancy, you're violating her body and spirit and she becomes alienated and inhuman, as happened to Tejerina. But it's not the child's fault, they say, and it deserves to live. But that's because they obviate the most essential fact. A fetus is not a child yet; its mother's love is the only thing that can make it into one. And a child is not a fully developed person yet; its caregivers' love is completely necessary for it. So again I ask, how can we force someone to love? But I also ask, how can we force a person to be born loveless? Isn't love an essential part of every human being? How can we even think that a person can be without love?

Now to conclude I want to depict the situation as I imagine it in Tejerina's head on the tragic day on which her child was born. She had just given birth in her house because she was hiding. Her pregnancy was unwanted so it was a shame for her to be seen in that state; therefore, she chose to have the child at home. It was born with her sister's help and then she was left alone with the child. At that moment she took it, that small creature who should arouse maternal instincts in her, but didn't. She actually hated it, or maybe she hated herself and didn't want that innocent creature to suffer from her lack of love. She was loveless; she was broken and she couldn't conceive of the idea of bringing a human being into the life she hated so much. But she was forced to, because abortion is strictly restricted by law in Argentina. Her pain was focused on that creature in front of her. She took it in her arms, giving it the only token of love that it was going to ever see. Then she put it into a cardboard box and carried it to the bathroom. There, on the bathroom floor, she laid it down and went to the kitchen for a knife. While she was away from the child, her alienation grew inside her. Her hatred towards the system that had violated her was only overcome by her hatred towards the child's father, a father in the mere biological meaning of the term. She was miserable and no one cared; they had actually put her into this situation: the father's child and society. She hated them all. Her hand tensed up when she grabbed the knife; she knew there was no other way. She'd premeditated her crime a hundred times, during her seven months of martyrdom. She'd been abandoned to her loss with a child in her womb; society didn't care about her or that child; it just cared about formalities. "So they think abortion is murder; I'll show them real murder then!" she said to herself. She went up to the child, but it wasn't a child anymore; it was the image of society and the child's father. She hated them, the society that had violated her body, forced her to carry an unwanted child for seven eternal months, ironically doing the same that the child's father had done to her: violated her, raped her and abandoned her to her loss without caring about her or her child. So she stabbed them, the father and society, but they'd never suffer as she did, so she stopped. Now she had finally aborted her child, and she felt the same as before:

loveless, but her martyrdom had only begun. And to the experts in
justice, this was only a mitigating factor.

A perfect love story

How many times have I read White Nights? I'm not sure. I'd say
enough times to have this story imprinted on my mind. Is it a perfect
romantic story? Yes, it is, because what is more romantic than
someone who can't get over a truncated love? What's more romantic
than lifelong suffering? But now we aren't talking about the perfect
romantic story but about the perfect love story, so I'm forced to
revise Dostoevsky's masterpiece.

I was walking over Most Biskupa Jordana, as I usually did when I
couldn't get myself to sleep. The Poznanian summer night was fresh
and the serene view was exhilarating. As usual, I was spending my
summer in the city; what should I go somewhere else for when I was
already somewhere else? Poznan was my adventure; everything was
new to me there, even though I'd been living there for more than
three years. A great percentage of the youth had gone back to their
hometowns, maybe out of remorse for abandoning their parents, and
those Poles who could get days off from work chose to go abroad, so
the night was full of early sleepers whose sleep was full of tiredness
from work and void of dreams. The wind, however, blew this
charged atmosphere away and left only the placidity of the empty
night, so empty that it invited me to fill it with wild adventures. And
what could be wilder than strolling around Katedra and across the
lovers' bridge, whose bars were heavy with padlocks left as tokens of
fervent love? I wonder about the ritual of that custom. If I were to do
that, I would surely take the keys with me and, after having locked
the padlock in the company of the woman of my life, I would throw
the keys into the waters so the Warta could hide them in its bosom
forever. Then a divorce would be very difficult because I would have

to dive down into the dark waters and try to unearth the keys from wherever they were. "That's a lifelong deal!" I thought, and I sneered at Church and civil marriages that could be dissolved with such relative ease.

I was lost in these thoughts when I saw a female figure leaning on the parapet of the bridge. I walked towards her, my heart beating faster, as her beauty revealed itself in front of me. I saw she was crying so when I got to a prudent distance away, so as not to scare her, I asked her, "Can I help you?" Of course, she didn't answer. She was startled by my sudden intrusion into her sadness. My presence was as unexpected as unwelcome. She stared at me, however, not with fear but with deep annoyance. I saw in her eyes that she had nothing to lose, but she would be glad to inflict some harm on someone. Fortunately, I was there and I was happy to put myself at her disposal, because I didn't have much to lose either. I said, opening my heart all at once, "Please let me help you; I'd feel useless if I can't. You see, we're here at a ridiculous hour in a place that's only visited by idlers and blind lovers. I wasn't expecting any company when I came here, but I found you and I can't help feeling it's destiny. You're crying and, despite the fact that we don't know each other, I already feel that your pain is my pain and I couldn't live with the idea that I abandoned a part of my soul on a desolated bridge. So I repeat, would you please let me help you?"

She only smiled, but it was more than I could expect. Tears were still running down her face, but they now looked like warm tears of happiness. The illusion was perfect: For some seconds I saw a beautiful girl, smiling at me and crying. It was too much for my voluptuous heart; I fell in love immediately. Now I needed to know who this girl was that I was meant to love; I needed her to start telling me everything about her, while I listened in silence. But she didn't utter a word. My heart started battering my chest, but I didn't know how to make her reveal herself to me. After some seconds of utter confusion, I said, "What's your name?" and for the first time I heard her voice: "Malwina". If a crow had come out of her throat, I wouldn't have minded because my feelings for her were already cemented, but what I heard was the most beautiful sound I'd ever dreamed of. Her voice didn't thrill nor was it high-pitched; it was deep, but extremely feminine. I introduced myself and she didn't seem to care about anything I said, but she put up with it as if she had no other option. Once in a while, she stared for a long time at the waters and I knew everything I said during those lapses would be carried away by the wind, but I didn't want to stem the flow of the conversation because I felt it was the only thing that linked us at that moment.

After a while, however, I just lost courage and became silent. I gave up, yes! Can you believe it?! I gave up on love at that moment, and it's the most shameful thing I've ever done. But she wouldn't allow me to fall so low; she said, "Would you walk me home?" and we walked silently to her door. When we arrived, I asked her, "Could I see you again?" and then she told me, "I like you, but it's complicated. When you found me, I was crying for my boyfriend. We are apart and our love is impossible, but I love him, I love him with all my heart. I like you, but I don't want to make you suffer as I'm suffering now, from unfulfilled love." "I'm suffering already," I said. "You wouldn't believe how fast two kindred souls may reach a communion of feelings, but it's true, I could swear on my life, it's true! And I learned it today, when I saw you. If you don't feel the same, then I'm just a fool, but I feel we're meant for each other." She sighed and said nothing. My heart stopped beating for some seconds, or maybe it was just vibrating so fast that it felt like a still string which could snap under the slightest tension. I couldn't utter a word if my life depended on it, so I was just waiting for the coup de grace to go home and assimilate all the feelings of the night. But she said, "I feel the same for you. Since I saw you, I felt a strange comfort in my soul, as if I wasn't alone anymore." Oh, Malwina! How happy you made me at that moment! How could I ever pay you back for such a gift?! I said to you that night, "You don't have to be alone anymore, because I'll never leave you." And you smiled and I was the happiest man on earth.

We went on meeting and the subject of your boyfriend was never touched upon. I was happy with that arrangement because my heart couldn't possibly deal with the idea of losing you. I preferred to believe we were in a romantic limbo, in a love nest built of ethereal branches on a peak unreachable to anyone else. You gave yourself completely to me, or maybe my feelings for you enshrined you in tenderness and enthusiasm, so I never saw your doubts, your pain, the hole in your heart. But everything comes in cycles and our relationship was reaching the starting point anew. After two weeks of Heaven, you mentioned the inevitable: Your boyfriend was coming to visit you. I didn't want to believe in his existence; not after all the days I had seen your happy face in front of me. For a moment, I thought that we needed just one last strenuous emotional effort to banish him from your life; he seemed so surreal to me at that time. But since you gave me the news, everything which seemed so real before started fading away, so fast that in no more than a week I knew for certain that our love would never be.

Now, if I stopped the story at this point, it would be romantic, but it wouldn't be happy, and my definition of love implies happiness. Now love is not a feeling but action. Love cannot be spoken and it can be felt only by the person loved. We can't feel that we love someone; that's absurd to me. However, we can feel loved by someone and we can try to reciprocate that love or to share that love with others. If you asked me to put it simply, I'd say: Love is care. Now comes the convoluted part of every romantic story. When I met Malwina, I was single, but it's never so simple. In my case, it was as simple as it can get, because it had been a long time since I last fell in love, so I was ready to invest all my feelings in a new relationship. However, there were some friends and ex-girlfriends to who I owed some explanations. Some people are discrete and choose not to say anything until it's so evident that there's nothing to say, but that's not my style. Whenever I was in front of my friend I felt the way she looked at me implied the fact I was single, so I felt cheap not to tell her that I'd met someone. With my ex-girlfriend, it was a little different because she actually asked. It was subtle; I'd had an accident and she asked me, "Is there someone to take care of you? A girlfriend?" Well, it wasn't so subtle, but I must give her some credit for taking advantage of every opportunity to inquire about my civil status. I also told my mom, but that was just because I'm expansive and I have a friendly relationship with her. Anyway, the point is I was betting hard on Malwina because I felt really confident about her. She is so sensitive that I would've never thought she could get lost in her own feelings. I've gotten lost in mine sometimes, but not for long, and I never regretted a decision or opened a door that was already closed. Not that I didn't try; it just never worked for me because, in the end, I found myself in the same place as before. Our minds play tricks on us and sometimes bring back vivid memories of parts of our past lives, but those are just Hollywood movies, made up of the best scenes; they are pure image without text between the lines, without substance. I'm not saying we can't try again with someone from our past, but it shouldn't be based on memories because they are deceitful. If we happen to find an ex-partner in our lives again, we can start to build all anew, but we shouldn't count on past feelings, because they've surely changed already. But our minds are sometimes so vain as to believe they can erase the part of our lives in which we were apart from the other person and that we can just return to our previous relationships. We believe that we can catch up with everything, obviating relationships with other people and events that transformed us completely. Our characters always remain, that's true, but circumstances are the greater part of love: Real love, not the thrill we have when our eyes or minds are flattered. Love happens naturally like everything else in the world; love is no fight but a surrender. Love is here and now; it's not in plots or future projects but in the reaction to our present situation. I had burned my bridges for Malwina, but love was there to save me. In the darkest moment, when I realized everything was over between us, a stranger approached me in the street. However, she seemed to know me, and after a few seconds I recalled her too. "You're Ewa, right?" I said. We had been at the same party two weeks before and we had talked for a while. Talking to her back then had been uneventful, but now I couldn't help seeing that she was very attractive and had beautiful features. Back then I hadn't even paid attention to the fact I was talking to a beautiful girl, but now it all came back to me as if in an epiphany. Back then I hadn't noticed her eagerness to talk to me, but now I noticed. I asked for her number and we've been in touch since then. What happened to Malwina? I don't know, but to let her go without hindrances was real love on my part. Now my need for giving love is once more appeased, since Ewa seems to accept all I want to give her. Is this not happiness? Even if it ends one day, right now I'm just happy all my love didn't go to waste; that it found someone who gladly accepts it.

The fake glasses

Romantic stories are condemned to be uninteresting for people who have never felt some kind of strong emotion, but, for many, this story will sound familiar.

I went to work that day, as on any other, trying to focus on the interesting part of my job rather than on the numbing one. A lot of Tao reading had made me at last accept work as part of life and taught me not to be overly ambitious; to perform to my best abilities all the tasks I was charged with and not to betray the trust my colleagues had in me. In that way, although my job was far from being my dream job, I was satisfied with myself at the end of the day. I left to others the task of wondering whether the work we did at my company was meaningful or not; I felt fulfilled as long as money was deposited in my bank account every month. And I used that money to buy products and services that were provided by other people who were thus satisfied with their jobs too. The circle was completed that way and I felt in communion with society.

However, I felt lonely. I´d never been outgoing or really funny and I didn't compensate for this dull personality with my looks either. Therefore, I was imbalanced; there were women who loved my sensitivity and tenderness, but I was never able to settle for them. I wanted real, sparkling, effervescent love, and not the conventional, sedate, laid-back version. So I decided to do something about it. Now, you need to bear with me for a moment because what I'm about to tell you may sound too fantastic for your auditory organs. Since my early teens, I'd had these eyeglasses with fake lenses, which I kept somewhere in a box and never used. These weren't prescription glasses; I just bought them at a glasses store one day to try to look more intellectual, but I never wore them for more than an hour because they felt cumbersome. However, from the few times I wore them in public, I knew that there was something extraordinary about them. Whenever I wore them in front of girls, I felt they looked at me with more eagerness, as if I were more attractive.

I´d never taken advantage of this supernatural quality of the glasses because I didn't feel it was honest to wear glasses without a prescription. I equated it to pretending to be blind or deaf, which could be insulting to real blind and deaf people. However, recently I ignored my moral qualms and decided to make good use of the glasses. I would see if they worked in the long term or just superficially. I didn't mean to use them to seduce every single girl I fancied but to find the one, even though she would be under the spell of the glasses and not really attracted to me. But I decided to try without thinking too much about the consequences. So I put them on one evening and went to my favorite bar. I must admit I didn't feel the same effect I had felt years before, when I had worn them in front of teenage girls. Maybe the effect faded as girls developed their minds, I thought. However, I did see some pretty girls resting their interested eyes on me and even a baby smiled when I passed by it. Once in the bar, I took a look around and in a few seconds I spotted a beautiful girl, who I wouldn't have ever hoped would be attracted to me were it not for the glasses. She wasn't looking in my direction, so I approached her, confident in the power of the glasses. And I wasn't wrong; she looked at me with a look I'd seldom seen: It was the look of desire. She was even more beautiful from close up. Everything felt so genuine and by the end of the evening I had almost forgotten I still had my glasses on, but I remembered when we were saying goodbye. She wanted to see me again and looked really interested in me, and I would've taken my glasses off to see whether the effect of the glasses was permanent or whether it wasn't the glasses but me, but I couldn't. I was already afraid of losing her. Yes, dear reader! I had just met her and she was already more important to me than reality itself! Yes, I was a coward! Yes, I preferred to deceive myself than to miss the chance of seeing her again! Say whatever you want, there's no insult or injury which I haven't thought of already.

This compunction haunted me during the days that elapsed before our next meeting. It was the guilt of knowing that I was harming no one else but myself; I was my own victimizer. It was a vicious circle that could only be broken by taking off the glasses, but I couldn't; I simply couldn't. Now I wore them everywhere, for fear of breaking the spell that kept her attached to me. I didn't know exactly how the glasses worked. What happened if she saw me by chance in the street? Would she recognize me? Would she see my real self? Would she like me still? I didn't want to risk it. We spent a glorious afternoon together; its glory lay in its simplicity. We'd walked around my favorite park and then, sitting on a bench, I kissed her warmly. No fancy special effects that ruin the scene; only pure romance. Again, the hour of departure, and again my cowardice. But this time I couldn't resist, my nerves were racked and I felt I wouldn't survive the incertitude any longer. I took off my glasses in front of her and what happened next convulsed my sanity. The tenderness, passion and affection in her look hadn't changed but she had changed. She wasn't beautiful anymore but plain looking. It was another version of her, with less delicate features and rougher corners. The color of her eyes, hair and complexion were the same, but her silhouette had changed as if it were out of focus, as if I were looking at her with the wrong lenses. And that was it; I instantly understood it all. I wouldn't go to the opticians or try to fix my eyes. I threw away the glasses; I had no use for them now. In a second, I learned to look at the girl in front of me. Her rough features became ever sharper till I saw her full beauty again. She was the beauty I had captured with the lenses of my eyes, and I was as proud as a good photographer can be.

The perfect romantic story

I'm a writer and I believe in fiction only because it's the best way of conveying our deepest feelings. There's elasticity of expression in fiction that allows for more thorough explorations of our emotions, something that can't be done in nonfiction genres. Because at this precise moment the reader doesn't know if it's the writer who's speaking or one of his characters, but the tricky part is that the writer doesn't ever know for sure either. Because life is about taking stands and defending them, even if we change sides later on. There's nothing wrong with inconsistency, but there is with spiritlessness and indifference. Because there's nothing indifferent about life, we're always forced to go on. As in a chess game, we must always move and hope we won't make an irrepairable mistake. That's why I personally don't have anything against people who defend their ideas against mine, but I strongly dislike sceptics who think they can just avoid certain issues by being neutral about them. Unfortunately for them, there's nothing more absolute than truth, so the fact they choose a middle point just makes them wrong, and there's nothing wrong in being wrong, if you're honestly convinced that you're right, but not caring about the truth is simply despicable.

And I could mention many of these sceptical attitudes by which people default on life, but I'll just mention one to exemplify. Although we know we're unique, we have our own fingerprints which we share with no one else in the world, and although we generally behave as if we were the center of the world and everything that happens to us is by default the most important thing in the universe, there are some people that still like fumbling with the idea of other universes or multiple realities. Some people, who the same day were crying over their domestic tragedies and were so absorbed by their own problems and needs that they forgot to feed their dogs or throw out the garbage, now are saying that there might be a chance that they exist in another time and place. So why all the fuss earlier in the day then? If they exist somewhere else, why should they suffer in this shitty reality? The only answer I can find to this conundrum is that it's because it's the only reality we have, as shitty as the thought may be for many people. The same goes for our universe, and if there are multiverses, as some scientists may argue after one their sessions of mental masturbation, it's totally irrelevant to us, who, by definition, aren't affected by other universes. But I'm digressing, since my aim is to write the perfect romantic story. So let me start.

Life is a chess game, or rather chess is like life, but for chess players who already have a good handle on chess, but are still far from understanding how life works, a chess game is rather a good metaphor. However, there's a very important factor in which chess and life differ completely: chance. While in chess it's all about planning and projecting moves, in life there's so much randomness that sometimes it makes all our plans futile. The chess metaphor would be more accurate if, instead of considering ourselves the chess-masters who move the pieces, we thought of ourselves as simple pawns who, although they believe they're making a deliberate decision that only concerns them, are actually part of a bigger plan. But then, who is the chess-master for non-religious people like me? The answer is: all of us together are the chess-master. We're like random thoughts in a chess-master's head, but it is up to us to get synchronized with other thoughts to form meaningful movements. And at this moment, I'll ask you to allow me to indulge in the metaphor of the chess game for the sake of the story.

So in my illusion of being in control of the game, I went always forward, not without thinking carefully, to a greater or lesser degree, about every one of my actions and generally analyzing the results. Thus, I developed the fantasy of learning how to live and make the right decisions. My instinct for justice staunchly defended the conviction that we receive our just deserts and, therefore, justice is eventually done if we behave honestly. Nowadays I still believe in honesty, but I'm not that sure about this individual justice we believe in. I think it's rather a communal justice that doesn't correlate directly to our individual actions. So what I'm saying is that I believe that the goodness or badness of our actions have no effect on our destiny or, following the chess metaphor, on our game because for the sake of the game some pieces must be sacrificed and what seems to be a bad move may actually be decisive for the final result. So the chance element consists of the fact that we don't know how the other pieces will move, so what may be considered a bad action from our narrow point of view could actually be beneficial to the game. To sum up, life is extremely unfair.

That was my case. I've had my share of bad experiences. I was barely eighteen when I met my ex-fiancee. We met as classmates at university and during the semester we became friends. I found her attractive the first time I saw her, but it took more time for her to get used to my odd handsomeness. I'm a tall ungainly guy with an unremarkable physiognomy. My facial features exist for mere physiological purposes and they play no aesthetic function at all. I have nondescript brown eyes and hair and a boringly pale complexion. I don't have any outstanding defects, which makes me simply plain and very hard to remember by sight. Now, my ex-fiancee is not a beauty, but she captivated me with her outgoing character and sensuality. She was my first girlfriend and I concentrated all my romantic emotions on her, eagerly, blindly, desperately, senselessly. It's hard to believe, for someone as romantic as me, that a small detail can topple a seven-year relationship, but it did. She's a fervent catholic and I'm not a religious person; we'd managed to reach a compromise in every single practical aspect of our lives but one. She wanted me to get baptized and confirmed so I could marry her in a church. It broke my heart to refuse her a proper wedding, but I couldn't force myself to go and do something half-heartedly, even when my future happiness was at stake. Although I don't believe in any religion, I have a deep respect for religious leaders and churches and I couldn't cheat them. They always demand a proof of faith, be it explicit or implicit. They ask you to say or do something which implies that you believe in their god and I simply couldn't perform such an act without really believing; that would be the worst possible profanation I could imagine and out of mere respect to them as human beings, I couldn't possibly do that. But my ex-fiancee couldn't cope with the idea of a churchless wedding, so she broke up our engagement and left me. So I found myself 26-years-old and with no marriage prospects, which would be normal for many people at that age, but was depressing for me. I didn't like going out, but I forced myself to go to clubs and events where I could potentially meet the woman of my life, or the second such woman in my case. And I met one, Wirginia. Her character was as odd as her name. She was a painter who worked as a bartender in a cafe where I usually went for some social events. She found my shyness adorable, she told me, and I guess she found me reliable too, since I didn't flirt with any girl, much as I wanted to. So we hit it off and in a few months she was living with me. Like most artists, she was an interesting mess, and she was moody too, I mean, more than women in general. Now it's the time to confess; I'd never been with a girl I was really in love with. I didn't think my ex-fiancee or Wirginia were the prettiest women I'd seen. Every single day, walking down the street to my office, I could see a dozen girls as pretty as them and a few who were even prettier. I'm not saying we should all be convinced that our girlfriends are the prettiest women on earth and constantly verify it by comparing them to every single girl; quite the opposite, what I mean is, when we're in love, we stop searching because the woman in front of us is all we need, and I'd never felt like this about my girlfriends. I'd had this feeling, however, towards a few girls in my life, but I never had the good luck to have my feelings reciprocated. That's how, at the age of 27, I found myself in an empty relationship, but I was totally satisfied with it. Don't misunderstand me, we had plans together and I was faithful and dedicated to her, but the feeling of wonder wasn't there. That feeling which we have when a beautiful and interesting person chooses to be with us, like winning the lottery, yes, that's the best example. Not because of the money, that's actually a terrible example, but because of the gratuitousness of the prize. Thus, a mixed feeling of glee and guilt is born in us and it makes us better people. We feel that life has been too generous to us and, when we see the distress around us, we feel we need to give something back and we care more about other people.

But, although idealistically I thought that feeling exists, I'd never felt like that myself, and I was already resigned to a pragmatic life, where you need to "fight for the relationship" and make it work, in spite of the adversities. But then life gave me a new chance.

Wirginia told me she wasn't in love anymore and she left me. I must admit at that moment I didn't see it as an opportunity but as a curse; I felt I was doomed to loneliness and the mirror told me I was never going to find a beautiful girl who could reciprocate my feelings. I always believed in karma and my experiences had convinced me that I'd never be with a beautiful girl; I thought it was my divine punishment for being superficial.

Then I met Elena. What are the odds of meeting a girl like her; I don't want to dwell too much on it for fear of believing it's just an illusion. She's beautiful and intelligent and the fact of having been rejected by girls ten times less pretty than her gave a surrealistic aura to our first meeting. I had gone out that night because a friend had invited me for drinks. I saw some attractive girls during the night, but I wasn't in the mood for wasting my time on girls who I'd never seen again, as was usual when I met someone in a bar. Now, I don't know how to dance, but I always thought it is the best way to meet someone. There's something animalistic about dancing; it's a primeval state in which everything is legitimate. It's martial law for social conventions. How else can you easily approach a girl, grab her by the waist and ask her whether she fancies you or not? So for the first time I went to this popular club I knew about. However, I didn't dance with anyone; I was intimidated by the display of hormones on the dance floor. After an hour of walking around with a beer that I barely managed to finish, I decided to go home. And there she was, sitting alone in front of the entrance, the most beautiful girl I could imagine, or rather, beauty itself, if it could be captured in one image. Not even for a second did I think that something could happen between us, but, I don't know why, I retraced my steps and asked her, "Hi, are you OK?" She answered me, "Yes, just breathing some fresh air." "Have you been to the club?" I asked, more boldly this time. "Yes, that's why I needed some fresh air," she said. "I'm a regular here, but today I didn't feel like dancing."

Now, dear reader, you can draw your own conclusions, but I'll give you mine anyway. We're married and have two beautiful kids. I always wonder at the fact that the only day I decided to go dancing, she stayed outside. If she'd been inside, I'd probably not have met her, but she was outside that day on which, by a mysterious impulse, I went to that club. Now, coming back to the chess metaphor: Life plays chess with us. It may seem that we're going to lose the game, but, in a gambit, everything is overturned. What seemed to be a terrible situation now is the condition for our victory. Maybe I had victory at hand at other times; maybe I just chose to see the chance this time and I closed the game. That doesn't take away from the fact that this chance was given to me in spite of my merits, in the same way as a pawn in a chess game sometimes has the chance to take the queen.

The perfect crime

I've never liked crime fiction; I think it lowers the status of literature to mere sports, something we do to pass our free time and get a thrill when we're bored. Mind you, I've read the whole Sherlock Holmes collection and really enjoyed it, but I think the novelty died with Conan Doyle and, in my view, whoever started plagiarizing this good writer and creating a whole genre from his work should be deemed as one of the antichrists of literature.

Now that I've made clear my opinion about crime stories in general,

I'll tell you my own crime story. But in case there may be some among you used to the thrill of finding out who, why and how, I promise to spoil their fun by giving away all the mystery from the very beginning. Thus, only those who enjoy real literature will remain and listen carefully to what I have to say. So, basically speaking, I'll tell a crime story from tail to nose.

In a regular detective story you know the crime, but you don't know the perpetrator, their motives or their means. Now, as I mentioned before, it's my own crime story, so who better than I to be the criminal. My motives are jealousy, general despondency, disillusionment and bitterness, to sum up: a broken heart. The means, her blind trust in me, her carelessness bordering on stupidity, the fact that we've shared a bed for almost six years, the fact that she is soundly asleep and I'm not. I mean, what else do you need? A weapon? Wouldn't two healthy hands suffice? And what about all the rage suppressed inside me? Isn't that more lethal than a kitchen knife or a gun? But I didn't lie when I told you I'd start from the very end of the crime. We all know that the climax of a detective story is the reconstruction of the events that make us relive the very moment in which the crime was committed. So that moment is now, on this bed in which I lie staring at the ceiling. Beside me, the warm body of my fiancee, whose placid sleep hasn't been disturbed by the knowledge of the harm she's done to me. But, as many people have said before, life is a chess game, and I'm a step ahead of her because I know what she's done, but she doesn't know that I know. The crime will be committed as soon as I finish my story, and there won't be a way back.

Our first meeting was at a club and it was an explosion of emotions. It was one of her friends' hen parties and while we danced, I asked her when she was planning hers and that's when I saw for the first time her sweetly sardonic smile. We danced the whole night and I stole a rose from the fancily decorated bar, hid it up my sleeve and presented it to her. I truly believe the first magic trick was born like that. We were so passionately in love with each other, then so tenderly and finally so steadfastly. Everything evolved as in a psychology manual; love went from a blazing flame to smoldering firelight, but it seemed it would never be extinguished.

Up till last night, when she went back to her hometown for another friend's hen party. It was a good occasion for her to visit her family too, and I was happy for her. But life seems to come in cycles, which in her case are marked by friends' weddings. She met me on the eve of the marriage of a friend of hers and now the cycle has started all anew. I remember she was drunk when we met. She'd danced the whole night with me and we ended the night at my place. I still remember her startled face when she woke up. It was three seconds of total disorientation followed by a self-deprecating smile. She'd talked for an hour to her friend to convince her there was nothing to worry about and she was perfectly fine. Fortunately, no one had called her mother.

She got drunk again at the party last night. She told me her innocuous version of the story, in which she ended up at her friend's house, sleeping on the living room sofa. But this evening, when she was already taking a shower at home, I heard a message notification on her phone. I'd never read her messages before or even dared to fumble with her phone, but something told me there was no legitimate reason for her to receive a message on that day and at that hour. I lifted the phone to my eyes and I first looked at the sender's name: not registered. My heart started beating violently and a feverish cold ran through my spine as I read the message: "I'm Christopher. I'm sorry, I took your phone number while you slept and forgot to tell you. I'm dying to see you again. Are you still in town?"

Of course, I didn't react immediately. What could I have done that wouldn't be stupidly murderous? I mean, does she deserve having me go to prison for her? Hatred and revenge have simmered in my heart for the last few hours. Now that the other feelings have cleared away, I'm resolute at last. My heart is filled with a homogeneous feeling that I dare call justice. And justice will be done tonight, while she sleeps her carefree sleep. The story is finished so I don't have any other reason to delay the crime. I enter into a trance, similar to the kind ancient assassins slipped into before fulfilling their duties. I'm barehanded; I don't need any weapon for the harm I'm going to inflict. I take a last look at her, as I imagined her before I learned who she really was. A single act will end it all; it will shatter my illusions and leave a void inside me forever. But there's nothing else to do. Therefore, I commit the perfect crime, bloodless, without any violence, but with coldblooded determination. I shut my eyes tight and force myself to sleep. I've already deleted the ignominious message and blocked the number on her phone. We're planning to get married and we'll do it. One day, when she's be too old to start her life anew without me, I'll kindly let her know that I know what happened last night. I'm looking forward to seeing the look of utter despair followed by horror on her face.

A real woman

My name is Tomek and I'm thirty-three years old. I like strolling around Poznan early in the morning, but usually I can´t indulge in this pleasure because I need to rush to work. I'm a sleepyhead, but fortunately I have a fiancee that makes sure I´m always on time for work. She shakes me awake every morning and prepares my breakfast while I get ready. We met just a year ago, but I've realized that she's an angel and I couldn't possibly live without her.
But today is Sunday and I haven't had a care in the world for almost the whole morning. I must just return home at eleven to go to Church with Eliza, who says the only reason to miss Church is to be

prostrate in bed. On my way to the park, a young woman crossed my path and handed me something. It turned out to be a flier for a movie this afternoon. I had seen the young woman walk in my direction. I had seen her shapely body and her pretty face, and I was too busy looking at the curliness of her blond hair to see what she handed to me. Once my eyes fell on the piece of paper she had handed me I felt cheated. But it is worse than that; I feel outraged at having being treated as an ordinary male or, as women like to say around here, "zwykła świnia." Many offensive assumptions on the young woman's part come to my mind right now. The most flagrant one is her certainty that I would take the flier. She'd done her sexy walk in front of me, swinging her hips a little more than necessary for the health of her knees and putting on her best nonchalant face, without ever making eye contact. Then I realized what her reasoning might have been. She must have thought I was so spellbound by her charade that I hoped to get her phone number or a love message on that piece of paper; nothing farther from the truth. I had observed her beauty objectively and I realize some people may find it offensive when I look at them, but this is simply out of curiosity because it helps me elaborate my humanistic ideas. I was aware she was an attractive young woman, but my interest in her was by no means as base as she had presupposed it was. I was actually thinking what a well-dressed young woman may be doing strolling near Park Wilsona on a Sunday morning. The fact that she was attractive only added circumstantialities to her presence at that place and time, so I had wanted to capture every detail of her appearance. That was it. I'm not the kind of man that jumps at the first sexual opportunity he has, and this assumption outrages me, not because it is offensive to me in particular but because it is offensive to men in general, or at least to Polish men. I'm not sure what the reach of her assumption might be: whether she thinks only Polish men are "zwykłymi świniami" or other nationalities too. Anyway, I was surely not giving off any porcine vibe because I know I don't have a tendency to think of sex every seven seconds, as ordinary men are supposed to do. The only time I give free rein to my sexual desire is in front of my dear Eliza because she is the only one who deserves it.

She would never behave like this young woman has just done. She is too straightforward and too contemptuous of base behavior to be able to put on such an act. Her scorn would be so evident in her eyes that no man with indecent thoughts about her would be able to stand her look. That's the kind of woman I have beside me and not, quoting my dear Eliza, "Some modern girl whose head is as hollow as her values." And she proves it to me every day that she isn't like the rest. She cooks for me, washes my clothes, irons and places them in my wardrobe; she keeps the house impeccable and makes sure there's never a lack of provisions. That's where I come in, because I'm sent on daily errands to buy a bag of flour or sugar when we run out or to go to the supermarket with a long list of items scribbled on a piece of paper, much like a doctor's prescription. I've learned to ask if there are any words I don't understand because this may bring about a domestic tragedy like the one which is imprinted indelibly on my mind.

Once I hadn't checked the list before leaving and, when already at the supermarket, I couldn't for my life decipher one of the items on it, so I just skipped it. When I got home, I put away all the products and prepared myself for the domestic warmth Eliza had got me so used to. But she happens not only to be a very intelligent person but also to have a sixth sense, so when she went to the kitchen she asked me calmly but firmly, "Where is the parsley I asked you to buy?" "Oh, it was parsley!" I said, "I'm happy to know at last what that indecipherable word was." Only now when I look backwards in time do I realize my terrible mistake, but, as they say: hindsight is 20/20, and back then I didn't have the luxury of knowing what I now know. I was really insensitive at that time. As she explained to me later,

when she became calm again, I had neglected the only thing she
requested from me. She did all the chores, she took very good care
of me and watched over my physical and mental wellbeing. The only
thing she demanded in return was that I do the shopping, but my
negligence had destroyed the domestic paradise she'd so carefully
created for us both. This act of total indifference on my part had
severed the tender threads she'd so carefully woven between us.
When she explained this to me in a soft tone I understood her first
reaction. The good-humored smile that the discovery of the
indecipherable word had drawn on my face was mistaken for
mockery. Eliza then jumped at me swiftly and so violently that she
made me lose my footing. She fell over me and in only one minute
she left the bloody tracks of her nails all over my face and neck and
also on my clumsy hands that had broken two of her fingernails
while I was trying to defend myself. Probably because of the pain
from her fingers, she grabbed me by the hair and started banging my
head against the floor, whose carpet cushioned almost the whole
force of the impacts, as she explained afterwards; although my head
ached for a week, which was only my fault, she said, because I chose
to watch TV instead of resting.

When her legitimate anger was over, she excused herself and was on
the verge of tears, but I didn't let her humble herself. I knew it was
my fault and I promised never to be so negligent again, and we
closed that chapter for ever. The next day, I explained to my
coworkers that I had been attacked by a neighbor's cat, but when
they answered that that pet should be put to sleep I couldn't restrain
myself and shouted, "How do you dare to blame such an innocent
creature!? It was only my fault for being careless." Oh, Eliza, if they
knew the kind of woman you are; if they could see the purity of your
heart as I can see it. If I could tell them our story, they would
understand, but they aren't as sensitive as I am and they can't see the
goodness behind your actions. On another occasion, you showed me

how much you care about me. I was careless again, but this time my neglect was graver. We went to a party and I kept watching a woman while she was dancing. You remarked on my indecorous behavior once and that should've sufficed me, but I stared once again. I won't start again with my excuses about not watching her sexually but with humanistic interest. I know what I did is unpardonable and I'm just glad you forgave me. When we got back home that evening, you mentioned the fact that you had to remind me twice of my duties as a future husband. It was as embarrassing for me as it was for you, believe me, and I've never again dared to stare at a woman in your presence. But you were really upset and I understand why you took the chopping knife and held it to my face. You wanted me to realize the severity of my actions and it was the only way to open my blinded eyes. But at last I saw it all when you told me in a tearful voice that if I ever dared to think sexually of another woman, you'd kill me and throw my mutilated body into the Warta river, and if I dared escape with another woman, you'd burn down my mother's house with her inside. I know my mother trusts you unconditionally and even if I told her that you stabbed me once, she would just believe that I made that up to incriminate you. After all, she knows as well as I do that you're a hundred times more righteous than me and besides, you are both so close. I don't know exactly when you became so intimate, but there seems to be a bond between women that we men can't even start to fathom. Anyway, I wanted to avoid a tragedy so that day I gave way to your more than sensible proposition to marry, and that's why now I have the honor of being your fiance. Eliza, you know I'd never leave you, and you know your suicide threats were unnecessary. I'd never think of leaving you, my love, because you're a real woman, and I love you for that.

The little prince

Once, in Argentina, a land of hidden dinosaurs and unexploited natural wealth, there was a young boy who traveled a hundred kilometers to visit his grandfather almost every summer. His grandfather lived alone in a big house in the countryside and, although he had a large family, he seldom received any visits. Since his wife had died years before, he hadn't received many visits from his relatives. His sons had filial love for him, and they made sure he never lacked anything, but they had never become friends with him and had seldom a reason to go and spend time with him. His grandchildren, who hadn't been encouraged to spend time with their grandfather, didn't have the habit either and they rarely had free time to go and chat with the old man. But this little boy was the son of the old man's daughter, who loved her father unconditionally and constantly taught this love to her son. Every summer, she'd sent her son to spend time with his grandparents and later on, when he was a little older, she'd always suggested he should visit them.

That's why the little boy found himself almost every summer at his grandpa's. He'd learned how to play chess from him and they took almost two hours per game because he always thought carefully before making any move. His grandpa sometimes dozed off during games, but he always woke up when his turn came and, although he helped his grandson defend himself and hinted how he should attack, he never allowed him to win. This didn't discourage the little boy; on the contrary, it made him wonder about the immense knowledge hidden in that game and therefore in life too. It was as if a hole was open in the universe every time they played and through that hole he could glimpse the mysteries of the world.

Some afternoons the old man would sit his grandson on his lap and ask him to tell him about his dreams. "What do you want to be when you grow up?" he asked, and probably he didn't expect an informed answer such as an accountant, a lawyer or a doctor, but he surely expected something less nonsensical than what his grandson invariably answered: a prince. However, never a sign of disapproval showed on the old man's face and he always asked about even the smallest details of his grandson's dream. He'd ask what color his cape would be and whether he would wear a sword or a saber. He'd allow him to ride his cart horse so he'd know how to ride a steed when he got one, and his grandson would be exhilarated at those moments.

One day, when he was seven years old, the grandson went up to his grandfather and told him he needed a coronet if he was ever going to be prince. He didn't want a crown because he didn't want to be a king, but he knew princes wore small crowns called coronets. He cried the whole day and then he refused to talk about his dreams to his grandfather whenever he asked him about them. That summer was a gloomy one, but grandson and grandfather were fond of each other and they didn't allow the issue of the coronet to get between them. When the little boy was leaving for home, the grandfather called him to his room and gave him a golden coronet with gemstones that had cost him all his savings. He asked his grandson to keep it in a safe place and not to show it to anyone and the boy promised this, but he didn't understand why people shouldn't know that he was officially a prince now. When he got home, he remembered his promise, so he didn't dare to open his mouth, but he left the coronet in a visible place in his room. One day he heard his mother's shouts. He ran up to his room and there he saw her, holding up the coronet. He explained his grandpa had given it to him and that now he was a real prince while his mother just stared at him speechless. His father seemed at a loss what to do too, but he explained to his son that that was a really expensive piece of jewelry and that he wasn't sure it was correct to keep it. He called the grandfather on the phone, but he didn't get an answer to his predicament and in the end he just resigned himself to the fact that the old man had lost his sense of fairness and had spent all his money on a golden jewel, leaving his sons without any inheritance other than the house. He tried to persuade the old man to take the coronet back and keep it himself or sell it, but the only thing he got as an answer were threats to throw the coronet into the river if ever anyone dared take it away from the child.

Thus, everyone in the family got wind of the coronet incident and most of them disapproved of it. But to his sons the news came as a shock. They were upset at the fact that the old man had spent his savings on such a vain object. They criticised him for having made their mother support the whole family, which had forced her to be seldom home and to not have enough time to spend with her children. He'd lost his job in one of the country's crises and, as he wasn't educated enough and he was too old, he hadn't been able to get a new one. He'd sat at home doing nothing for years, because his patriarchal upbringing hadn't taught him how to cook or clean the house and his wife couldn't bear the pathetic sight of him trying to start learning it at such an old age. The daughter of the house had been in charge of most of the chores and she'd never complained about it. But later on, when they'd all moved out already, the mother had passed away and the sons couldn't help feeling that it was due to the strain of having supported a whole family by herself.

The stirring of bad emotions caused by the coronet issue made the old man fall into depression. He'd felt powerless when he'd been laid off and he felt the same now he had to live on the minimal pension granted by the state. He related to his grandson: he was an immigrant who'd come to the country looking for better opportunities and a new start to his troubled life. In his younger days, he'd imagined he'd be wealthy when he retired, and he'd be able to pamper himself and his family with comfort and luxury; after all, he'd always worked hard. But he'd seen his dream of wealth get ever more blurry, until nothing was left of it. When his grandson told him about his dream and his wish to have a coronet, he'd felt the hope he'd had when he first came to Argentina and he wanted his grandson to live out his dream for him. That's why buying him a coronet had made him so happy, because his grandson had felt what he'd always wanted to feel. A coronet would surely not make the old man happy, because he still lacked many of the things he needed to live out his dream, but it had been enough for his grandson to live out his, so he never regretted having bought it.

But now the latent guilt that he'd managed to bury in his heart had emerged and he became despondent and lost his appetite. In spite of all the care that his daughter gave him whenever she could go to visit him, the old man refused to abandon his house and go to live with her, and so he died one day. The whole family helped with his funeral and they were all truly sad about his death. But their affliction was compounded when it came to the disclosure of the will. The old man had left the big house to the little boy. Everyone felt the unfairness of this act, but they were also hopeless because the kid hadn't reached the legal age to do anything about it. So the sons just sighed and resigned themselves to the fact that the old man had wronged them in every possible way, but they never showed any resentment against the little boy.

Now, the boy, who had gotten used to telling stories about his noble adventures to his grandfather, didn't have an outlet for his imagination anymore, so he started writing down the stories that he'd told to his grandfather and invented new ones as well. That's how, with the passage of time, he became more and more interested in literature till he decided to become a writer.

When he was eighteen, he went to his oldest uncle and asked him to sign a contract with him. The contract made his uncle the owner of the big house, but also stipulated that he had to compensate his other siblings. His uncle signed the contract in sheer amazement and, after his nephew had left, he mulled over the whole situation for a long while. But that wouldn't be the last surprise the little boy would give him. When he went to the house and opened one of the bedroom doors, he saw the golden coronet lying on a bed. But when he called his nephew, he received the news that he'd gone away to try his luck in another country.

Years passed without any news from his nephew. His mother didn't want to disclose where he was or how he was faring, and the uncle's everyday affairs made him soon forget about the boy. Meanwhile, he'd managed the big house as well as he could. He'd consulted his siblings and they'd decided to rent it out to a couple that promised to take good care of it. The earnings were divided equitably among them. But he still didn't know what to do with the coronet. It was a valuable object which was probably worth more than a year's salary and all of them would have been able to put that money to good use, but he knew the symbolic meaning of this piece of jewelry, and he still respected his father's wishes and understood his nephew's dreams of grandeur. So he never told anyone that he'd found the coronet and he kept it in a secret place.

One day he was browsing the Internet and he remembered his nephew. He'd learned about the miracles of the worldwide web and he thought that there was no place his nephew could be that the Internet wouldn't find him. So he typed his name into a search engine and he got the biggest surprise of his life. His nephew was apparently a renowned writer and he was doing well in France, where he lived and wrote his books. He'd published seven books and some of them had very good reviews. He followed the links for some of them and bought their electronic versions. Their titles sounded familiar to him: "The Noble Heart", "The Vassal Prince", so he opened them. He was astounded by the dedication in all of them, which was the same. He downloaded all the books, even the recently published one: "Once There Was a Worldwide World," and he invariably found the same dedication, which he couldn't help reading with emotion in his eyes. It read: "To my grandfather, who taught me that to be noble I don't need a coronet."

My parents are alive

Based on historical facts
1999, Rosario, Argentina.
Elba was a happy 20-year-old girl. She lived in a nice flat near the university where she studied economics and she visited her parents almost every weekend. They lived in a big house in the rich neighborhood of Rosario. People say that money doesn't buy happiness, but Elba had good parents who provided for her physical and intellectual needs. Being well-off meant not only never having to worry about money or the future, it also meant a she had a good education and an environment that allowed her to cultivate her interests and find her vocation. She wasn't a bad person; she was simply a member of the higher class. She was what is called a decent person, and everything indicated that she was to become a very respectable citizen. She was responsible and conscientious in everything she did, and she was very polite and well-mannered, besides having nice features and always being well-dressed. All of it made her a more than agreeable person and a desirable friend. Of course, she looked down on lower-class people, not because they were poor but because they weren't cultured. There were some middle-class people in her circle of friends, but those were exceptional cases. The first time she made acquaintance with people who didn't have house servants and didn't vacation in Europe was at university. Before that she'd been shielded from the country's reality; so protected was she that she would deny fervently, whenever she talked to people abroad, that Argentina was unsafe or poor. In those situations, she would generally say, "Of course, there are poor people, but that's because they don't want to work and, with respect to the crime problem in my country, it's totally exaggerated; I mean,

I've lived there my whole life and nothing ever happened to me or my family." And it was true; her family managed to circumvent the daily violence and danger which the rest of the society lived in.

So everything was perfect in her life and "there was nothing she could dream of that couldn't be achieved by consistent effort" as her father would always tell her. He was a lieutenant colonel in the army and, although he'd inherited most of his wealth, he'd managed to keep it intact throughout decades of economic and political instability. His dreams of marrying a beautiful woman and sailing across the La Plata River in his own yacht were both realized, mostly thanks to his money, but also slightly due to the pleasantness and joviality he'd learned from years of idly socializing at private clubs, majestic parties and other events reserved for the higher class. However, a small annoyance marred his otherwise full happiness: people were upset at the country's military. He knew very well that the lower class were always jealous of the few people like him, who happened to be born into wealth, but he would have never thought that a nation could be ungrateful to its heroes. And, with all due humility, he considered himself a military hero. He had helped prevent communism from taking over his country and several times he had narrowly escaped being killed by subversive groups. The war against the Marxist guerillas had fortunately finished in 1983, when the Process of National Reorganization came to an end. Many communist supporters claimed that around thirty-thousand civilians had been abducted from their homes, tortured and disappeared by what they called "the repressive forces". He was simply outraged at these people's total lack of gratitude towards those that had saved their country from sinking into Marxist heresy. For a moment, at the period in which democracy had been reinstalled in Argentina and top military officers were being prosecuted, he had been truly concerned about his freedom, but so had the majority of military personnel, who organized a mutiny that forced the Congress to pass the Full

Stop Law, which stopped the prosecution of the rest of the people involved in the so-called state terrorism. The next law, the Law of Due Obedience, had been passed a year later simply to appease soldiers' consciences and restore some of their dignity. The law meant an amnesty for every soldier under the rank of Colonel, because they were supposed to obey orders. Thus, with the exception of two crimes – rape and extensive appropriation of real estate – soldiers had been reprieved from any punishment for their crimes. However, there was a third crime that had been left out of the deal because it was considered a continuing offence, that means a crime that's committed over and over again, and this was what worried him the most, although he didn't consider it a crime but an act of humanity. He managed to appease his fears most of the time, but whenever he heard or read news of someone being tried for this crime, his fears were stirred anew. However, the days of the power of the military were over, so he could do nothing to tie up any loose ends; he could only hope for the best. Everyone in his family knew about this situation, except for Elba. No one would have dared to tell her the truth because they loved her and they feared the truth would tear her heart.

But one day at the university everything changed for Elba. The life she knew was destroyed and she could never again put its pieces together. She was studying for an exam in the library of her faculty. She was alone, as was usual when she had an important exam to study for. She was so focused on her book that she didn't see the old woman who sat beside her and stared at her, convulsed by emotion. When she realized that someone was weeping beside her, she flinched away instinctively, but the fact that the old lady was staring at her startled her even more.

"What happened, Mam?" she asked. "What happened?" But the old lady didn't answer her. She repeated her entreaties – "Is something wrong, Mam? What happened?" – while she rubbed the lady's shoulder with her hand.

"Nothing's wrong," said the old lady at last. "I'm just so happy to see you."

This startled Elba even more. "Do we know each other?" she asked in a gasp.

"Oh, my darling," said the old lady, this time throwing her arms around Elba. But what paralyzed her with terror were the words the lady uttered in her ear, softly but clearly: "I'm your grandmother." Now, in normal circumstances these words have no horrific connotation, but Elba was sufficiently informed to be aware of the meaning these words had for a military child. "What are you talking about!?" she shouted in despair. "Get away from me!"

The old lady was dumbfounded; that was the reaction she had least expected. Although she hadn't been tactful in breaking the news to her granddaughter, she was utterly saddened by her reaction.

"I've been looking for you for twenty years," she said, her words muffled by her sobs. "I'm sorry; I couldn't find a better way to tell you, but you must believe me, you're my granddaughter. I'm totally sure. My poor son and his wife were murdered, but you're alive, you're alive!"

Elba couldn't stand it any longer. She put on the most composed expression she had and she said, "I understand your pain, but it doesn't allow you to shit on my family," and she left almost running, not even once turning her head back to see her grandmother's face covered in tears, her eyes a reflection of the desolation in her heart. Identity forgery and forced disappearance of minors were crimes punishable with at least three years in prison. Both her parents were convicted, in spite of her tears and sobs in court. She testified that they were the best parents a child could have and she added that, if the crime was committed against her, why couldn't she release them from their punishment? She never changed her mind, not even when she heard during the trial that her father was present at the moment of the execution of her blood parents and that it was at that moment that he had decided to take her home. How could she blame him or her mother? If they had wronged her in any way, they had already made up for it with twenty years of infinite love and support. But the judges didn't share her views and found both her parents guilty, condemning them to seven and eleven years in prison.

Elba never reconciled herself with the Argentinean judiciary system and, as soon as she finished her studies, she moved abroad, far away from the country that had robbed her of her parents. She never spoke to her blood grandmother either; she simply hated her for what she had done. She did speak with her father's mother, her "real grandma"; whenever she could she called her on the phone. She was also in touch with her aunts and especially with a cousin who she was very close to. She went back to Argentina every three or six months, so she could visit her parents in prison until they were let out. She also kept track of the news about other people tried for the same crime as her parents. She was astonished at most of the news. In one case, the convicted father repudiated his child and told him at the end of his trial, "This is all your fault. You've ruined our lives." In most cases, the children turned against their parents and sometimes they went so far as to demand the maximum penalty for them. Most of the children of disappeared people were glad to find their grandmothers, who had relentlessly looked for them. It was a great madness she couldn't understand, a Roman circus she despised with all her being. In Europe, where she was living, the few people who knew about this part of Argentinian history tended to compare the crimes committed by the Argentinean military with the atrocities committed by the Nazis in Europe. They found a real similitude between the abduction of minors in her country and the kidnapping and Germanization of Aryan-looking children by the Nazis in Europe. However, they took care never to stir the subject in front of her. By now she was already happily married with three children;

both her parents had already been released from prison and lived in a
secluded house in the countryside. She visited them once or twice a
year. Whenever some of her European friends or newly acquired
relatives were so tactless as to touch on the subject of her parents,
she would inexorably say, "I'm not a Nazi, but my parents are alive."
"The question is if a person who stole a newborn, who hid the fact
that the baby was robbed, who perhaps kidnapped or tortured its
parents, who separated it from them and its family, who always lied
about its background, who – more frequently than one would like to
think – mistreated it, humiliated it, deceived it; if a person who did
all, or some of, this can know and believe that this is parental love. I
answer no; that the bond with this type of person will remain
determined by cruelty and perversion." – the words of Maria
Eugenia Sampallo, the illegally adopted daughter of disappeared
parents.
The events depicted in this story are fictitious. Any similarity to any
person living or dead is merely coincidental.

The extra finger

Emi was almost never in the mood for laughing. She wasn't a
feminist, but she'd been raised without a father and when she was a
little girl she'd asked her mother why her brother had a penis and she
didn't and her mother had told her that all men have an extra finger
that helps them perform tasks women can't perform. She
remembered being outraged at this idea for a long time. When she'd
looked at her younger brother, she'd never seen anything
extraordinary in him. She'd never seen him use his magic finger,
even in situations which, in her view, certainly merited it. Many
times she'd demanded clarification about the magical powers of this
extra digit, but her mother just hissed her away, leaving her alone in
her quest to learn about its secrets. So she didn't actually know what

it could do when their mother's car broke down on their way to the theme park, or when her mother bought a kilo of mint ice-cream, her least favorite flavor, by mistake. In such cases, Emi stared at her brother with evanescent hope. He just stared back at her in puzzlement until she was convinced that there was something wrong with her brother's magic wand.

But that didn't discourage her in her resolution to find her grail; what actually shattered her illusion was a biology lecture at primary school. The penis, which her teacher tactlessly managed to compare to a big-headed worm for lack of proper pictures and without even waiting for the confirmation of the male students present at the lecture, didn't have any other magical features than getting women pregnant once it found its way into them. Of course, those weren't the exact words her teacher had used, but she was sure she'd understood the core of the matter. Now, this happened in the Twenty-first century, so it was impossible for her not to know that the way the not-so-magic worm got into women was through sex; therefore, she swore that that would never happen to her. And this was not because she hated babies; she loved those slobbering balls of baggy skin, but because she'd seen her mother juggle with work and domestic problems every single day, and she subconsciously imagined the same portrait of herself as a mother. Now, I repeat, Emi wasn't a feminist; she was just a real woman with worldly problems.

But this nuance didn't matter, because later on, when she got to a marriageable age, she was labeled as a feminist by guys who felt their maleness threatened by her. She was an idealist, and she'd never found a man who she could connect with emotionally, so she checked her sexual impulse whenever some guy happened to arouse erotic feelings in her. But also her personality worked as a shield against potential suitors. She was opinionated and outspoken, a combination that precluded her from many young men's hearts.

Some appreciated and even esteemed her sense of humor and insightful mind, but there happened to be no chemistry between them and her, so Emi's options for a potential partner were drastically narrowed. Thus, she fought loneliness with fits of crying, which she would have whenever she felt impotent to move on in life. She'd be seized by a violent desire to weep inconsolably, to abandon herself to this cathartic ritual. Because when she cried, she did it spontaneously, so her mind was free to objectify her feelings. Crying gave her a break from self-consciousness that allowed her to detach herself from her problems and see them as the normal hiccups everyone has in life. Because she'd tried the opposite too; she'd tried not having anything to cry about, and it was scary. She remembered feeling empty in her early teens, and wondering about death and suicide. Then she'd started taking stances in life and putting value on certain ideas and beliefs, which had actually made her who she was. So while her body cried instinctively, her mind rejoiced in the fact that she had something to cry about: she had values and ideals that were often crushed by people or revised by life, but she was glad she wasn't an empty vessel.

But her worst struggle began when she started caring about someone in particular. She didn't know it yet, because her conservative mindset didn't allow her to acknowledge her romantic feelings before the man in question made overt shows of interest in her, but she felt the pangs of life bursting out of her whenever she saw him. Then, one day he happened to declare his feelings to her, but the mechanistic way in which he expressed himself deeply disappointed her. She'd noticed his interest in her and she liked him for who he was, but what he'd just said sounded as if it had come from a sentient robot rather than a human being. There was no passion or enthusiasm in it; it was rather like a lecture on his biological and social needs, which included her. But he was more sensitive than she'd thought. When she sighed with frustration after his love declaration, he just looked at her full of understanding and said, "I know my words aren't romantic, but please make allowances for my nerves and the mess of thoughts and feelings this declaration entails for me. I still remember your story of the extra finger, which we've laughed so much at, and I want to tell you that I do have a magic finger that pointed me towards you. And its magic power consists simply in leading me towards my happiness. Now I'm happy and I ask from you to allow me to make you happy too." "Yes," she said, "but please don't take your happiness for granted because then I would feel idle in front of you, and I'd like to occupy myself with the pleasant task of making you happy too."

And that's how she stopped being a feminist, at least for one man in the world, and she became simply a woman, and when her daughter asked her why men have penises, she answered her that it was to get women pregnant, but that some men also have an extra finger.

The woman who woke up on a different day

She was woken up by the alarm. 7 am; just enough time to have breakfast and drive to work. Her boyfriend wasn't in bed anymore, which was strange because she always needed to wake him up. But more strangely still, there were covers on the bed. "Richard must have been cold last night, even though we're in midsummer," she thought, and indeed she felt it was too cold for summer. She opened the curtains and she was aghast by what she saw. The street was covered in snow and the trees were bare; it was evidently winter. She cried, "Richard!" but no one answered her. She ran to the kitchen shouting, "Richard where are you?!" but when she entered the room, she saw everything had changed. The furniture, the utensils and the appliances were changed; they looked more modern and expensive. "What in hell!" she said, and she ran back to her bedroom for her phone. There it was, on the bedside table, square and bigger than her hands. "What in hell is this?!" she cried in despair. She crouched down in front of the phone and stared at it listlessly, as if inventing a new kind of worship position. At last she touched it, grabbed it and eventually turned it on. It was a new iPhone model, like a miniature computer; the images were so neat and there were so many icons on the screen, so different from the minimalism of her old smartphone. She touched the calendar icon. It was what she expected, but she still gave a gasp of terror: January 2017. Last night, when she'd gone to sleep, it was June 2014. Just then, she went to the mirror and looked at her reflexion. Her haircut was different, and she looked slightly plumper, which actually suited her better; she might also look older, but she couldn't tell for sure. She would've stayed paralyzed the whole morning, trying to elucidate this mystery, but she was a practical woman and she was late for work. In the mental mess she was in at the moment, she had a single belief: No matter what the year, she needed to work to live. So she got dressed and drove as fast as she could towards the place that she supposed was still her work, not giving a second thought to the fact that her car looked slightly older. When she arrived there, she was relieved to see that, although her colleagues looked different, they still recognized her. There were many changes, though, the most important of which was that she'd been promoted to executive assistant. "At least some good news," she said, although she struggled to keep up with the pace demanded by her newly discovered tasks.

When work ended, she tried to make conversation with her coworkers, but she found herself at a loss for what to say, and their questions also seemed to come out of the blue for her. She just walked fast to her car and drove slowly home. She looked around to see if there were any changes in the city while her mind was clogged with theories of what might be happening to her. But she actually wanted to do the opposite of thinking and analyzing; she just wanted to get through the day without having to admit that she had a mental condition. Maybe when she woke up the next morning, she'd go back to the past. Looking at her new phone, she cherished the idea that maybe there was a reset button in her that was activated while she slept. She was looking forward to an evening of warm soup and movies, just to wile away the hours till sleep came. But when she arrived at her driveway, she saw another car parked in it. She thought of Richard and a spark of curiosity lit her spirit. "What would he look like? He had a handsome car; had he been promoted too? What would they talk about? Had they married?" She couldn't contain her emotions any longer and she started crying hysterically. She managed to put the key in the keyhole and open the door and, almost blinded by her tears, she managed to get to the kitchen. She just wanted some tea to soothe her nerves. While the water was boiling in the kettle, she heard some steps. "Richard!" she exclaimed, but the sound of the steps suddenly stopped. "Richard, come here!" she shouted pitifully, but there was no response to her plea. "Richard, please; I'm so scared! Please! Please!" she cried with a heartrending voice. And she plummeted to the floor, strengthless. But at that moment she heard more steps coming towards her. Her Richard was coming to rescue her from the madness she'd fallen into. "Oh Richard, save me, save me!" she cried, but her voice was suddenly strangled by the image in front of her eyes. "I'm not Richard, what are you talking about?!" shouted an angry voice that came from someone who didn't look at all like her boyfriend. "Where's Richard? What have you done to him?!" she shouted, while the rush of adrenaline made her recover all the strength she'd lost. "I don't know where he is. Why do you ask for him?!" shouted the voice in the same angry tone. She was so scared; she thought the man might be a hypnotist who was playing mind tricks on her. "Get away from me, demon!" she shouted. "Luiza!" he exclaimed, but now his voice showed mere anguish. "Calm down. You must be having a nervous attack. Calm down." But she sprang up when he tried to grab her arm. And she grabbed the kettle and hit him with it. The hot water splashed all over his lifted hand and hair, dripping down his face, some sprinkling her hand and clothes. He screamed in pain and she ran out of the house. She ran and ran until she couldn't run anymore, and there, in the middle of the sidewalk, she fainted.

She awoke in a hospital, and immediately cried for help. A doctor came in; outside she could glimpse two policemen guarding her door. "Miss Johnson," he said, "are you aware of your identity?"

"What?" she exclaimed.

"What's your full name?" he said.

"I'm Luiza Johnson," she said.

"And what happened yesterday evening?" he said.

"Someone broke into my house and I burnt him," she said, feeling that the police outside the door had something to do with that question.

"That someone is in intensive care in this hospital at this very moment; he received third-degree burns and has lost vision in one eye. He's also believed to be your boyfriend, Miss Johnson. According to some witnesses, you've been living together for over a year. Also, he says you were calling for your ex-boyfriend, who apparently you split up with around two years ago."

She gasped for air. It seemed as if oxygen was lacking in the air around her.

"Miss Johnson," the doctor went on. "We'll arrange some psychiatric treatment for you, but, inferring from your boyfriend's words and what you're saying now, I believe you have amnesia."

"That's not my boyfriend!" she cried, and she got out of the bed and ran to the door. The two policemen grabbed her by the wrists and shoulders and forced her back into the room while the doctor fled outside.

"Call the psychiatric ward," he shouted to a nurse, "and tell them we have an urgent case!" While inside the room she shouted and banged the door, "I'm not crazy!" could be heard from outside. "Let me go! I didn't know he was my boyfriend. Let me go!" But the policemen remained impassive outside and the hospital staff went on with their routine.

Stopover in Frankfurt

Based on real facts

Thiago had been waiting for this day for a long time. Back in Curitiba, he'd contacted a Polish university and they'd told him he could study there; he just needed to pay a fee because he wasn't European. He'd always wanted to live in Europe, and Poland had seemed a good option to him. He'd found a cheap ticket for a flight from Sao Paulo to Warsaw, with a stopover in Frankfurt. The air company was Condor, a German company that offered one way tickets for half the price of round trip tickets, which was something rare in air travel, even though it sounded totally fair. So he'd checked the off-season prices and had got a flight ticket for 400 euros, and that's how his dream of living in Europe had started. He knew he'd have to incur more expenses once he got to Poland. For one, he'd have to pay for his studies, but he was already paying in Brazil, as he'd opted for a private university that offered him better services than the public ones. He was by no means a rich guy, but his parents supported him financially and they helped him in every way they could.

He hadn't signed any documents yet because he preferred to do it in person, but he was in contact with the university. He hadn't applied for a visa either because, in that case, he'd have to wait for it in his own country. It was much easier to go to Poland and process his visa there, since he was entitled to a three-month visa-free period in the Schengen area, so that was the plan.

He went from his city to Sao Paulo by bus and, once at the bus terminal, he took a shuttle that went directly to the airport, although its fare was six times the amount of city bus tickets. At the airport, he saw that, as expected, he'd arrived eight hours before departure. He found a relatively comfortable chair and used this excessive amount of free time to try to finish Paulo Coelho's *O Diario de un Mago,* which he wasn't finding very interesting. He'd liked *O Alquimista* and *Veronica Decide Morrer,* but the book he was reading proved that you can never trust an author to write a good book. Two hours before departure, the check-in started and he was soon waiting in the departure area. Unfortunately, they hadn't allowed him to bring his bottle of coke with him so he needed to buy a new one. At the shop, an Argentinean guy started talking to him; something related to the book he was reading. He was always amiable, like most Brazilians, but the Argentine caught him unawares and it took him some time to get used to his lazy pronunciation of the Portuguese nasals and his Spanish interference in his choice of words. When he finally started to make sense of what his interlocutor was saying, the topic was changed; the Argentine was asking him where he was going. Thiago explained his whole plan in simple words while he invited him for a walk; he needed to stretch his legs. When they touched upon the name of the company Thiago was traveling with, the Argentine made an ominous grimace and said simply, "I traveled with that company once." The word "once", accompanied by a dejected countenance, didn't particularly make Thiago expect a positive story, but he asked him, "What happened?" anyway.

"I was actually doing the same thing you're doing. I study in Poland now, and back then I also didn't have a visa and I traveled by this cheap airline," said the Argentine.

"Amazing," said Thiago, refering to the fact that both of them shared the same goal.

"Yes," continued the Argentine. "But when I arrived in Frankfurt, the police stopped me, as they stopped everyone else on that plane. I didn't see such a display of authoritarianism when I traveled by Air France to Paris or by KLM to Amsterdam. When I was without a visa, they usually just asked me where I was staying and I just showed them my hostel reservations. But in Frankfurt almost every person was taken away for interrogation. When it was my turn at passport control, they asked me strange questions such as how much money I had, what my whole plan for the journey was, why I didn't have a return ticket and why I hadn't processed my visa in advance. I mean, I could've answered all these questions by saying that I didn't have a visa or return ticket because it wasn't mandatory to enter the Schengen Area, and that what I did or didn't do during my visa-free period was my business, but I was really candid and explained my whole situation to that guy because his senseless questions inspired me with the fear of the unknown, as if the whole conversation were just a distraction maneuver to find out something he could use against me. But I felt clean so I opted to answer every question he asked honestly so as to finish as soon as possible; my next plane departed in one hour. To my surprise, he didn't let me go but he called two policemen who escorted me to a small room. They didn't ask me further questions, nor did they respond to my entreaty to let me go because I would miss my plane. They released me just fifteen minutes before departure and I ran like a madman, but the bus that took the passengers to the plane had already left. At first, I thought they were going to put me on another plane; I deduced this from the countenance of the woman at the check-in counter. But after a couple of phone calls, she calmly told me that the previous plane had arrived more than an hour before so the company wasn't responsible for me missing the second plane. I said I was stopped by the police, but she simply said that that wasn't the company's fault. She immediately offered me a last-minute flight ticket, which I assumed would be cheaper. I despised the woman for trying to sell me stuff to help me out of a situation her company was responsible for, but I just wanted to finally arrive at my destination and, I don't know why, the whole police affair instilled a fear of deportation in me, which I was happy to leave behind as soon as possible. So she showed me the way to another counter, where a man offered me a ridiculously overpriced ticket. While I struggled with the idea that airlines charge more for a place that is probably going to remain empty, I asked the guy to give me just a normal ticket. So I bought a not quite so expensive, but still very expensive, ticket for a flight to Poznan the next day.

Now I just had to wait. While I sat somewhere near a socket, a Mexican guy approached me and, after he offered me something to drink, we became airport friends. I saw a pretty girl nearby and I went to say hi; she happened to be a Brazilian girl going to Berlin in a few hours. The three of us hung out together and, after deciding we were hungry, we went for a walk to try to find a supermarket, which the Mexican guy said was nearby. On our way, we passed by the train station, which happened to be next to the airport, and, to my deep regret, I learned that a train ticket to Poznan would've cost me less than half the price of the flight ticket and that the train departed that same night. I cursed the staff at the airline company a lot more, who hadn't had the decency to tell me the train station was just a few steps away, but I just comforted myself with the idea that a couple of hundred euros was a small price to pay for my dream of being in Poland at last. On our way, we also met an Argentinean girl who was weeping inconsolably. When the Mexican guy asked her why she was crying, she said that her flight to Hamburg had been delayed and she needed to stay for one night at a hotel near the airport. From the way she was crying, I was expecting something more, like: and I won't make it to my German grandmother's funeral tomorrow, or: and I have to pay for the hotel, or at least: and I've just hit my foot against the door, but ... nothing. She was actually crying just because

her flight had been delayed and the air company had behaved decently enough to give her a hotel room with food included. 'Pampered higher class girl,' I thought, committing a pleonasm, 'whose idea of tragedy is to be delayed while traveling through Europe with a budget that would feed a whole family for at least five months.' And we just walked away. The next day I took my plane and, fortunately, I arrived in Poznan in the end. A year later I met a German girl to whom I told this story, and you know what she said to me? She said that it was my fault and that I should've booked two flights with more margin between them. We never met again."
Thiago was upset by the story. He hadn't thought of a possible delay once he got to Germany. On the airline website, it was written that he should arrive three hours earlier to go through customs for flights to the Schengen area and he'd actually arrived eight hours before. But he hadn't thought he could still have trouble at his stopover in Frankfurt; besides, the company had offered him these flights with just an hour-and-a-half's margin between them, and there was nothing he could do because those were promotional tickets. When it was time to board, he bid goodbye to the Argentine and got on his plane. He couldn't sleep, as was usual for him on planes, and he arrived in Frankfurt feeling worried. But nothing could've prepared him enough for what he saw once there. At the entry gate, there was an interminable queue of Brazilians being stopped by the police; all the Germans coming back home with a reddish suntan were gone in just a few seconds. He saw just a few Brazilians being let through, while the majority were escorted somewhere. When his turn came, he already knew what was going to happen. The conversation developed as if it had been rehearsed. Everything the Argentine had told him was happening to him now. He was escorted to a small room, where he heard a Brazilian man sobbing while he paid a €4000 fine in cash for both him and his wife. But there was a new element in the story, an element that really surprised him. A

policeman was asking him for a contact number for the university he'd applied to. He gave it to them and they called. At the same time, they introduced him to an interpreter who was going to translate the questions they'd ask him. Apparently, the previous policeman hadn't understood him well and an interpreter was required. They told him this would cost him a hundred euros and he refused to pay, but they remarked that, if he didn't accept, they'd simply deport him. They called the Polish embassy and he heard an argument between them; the German police were refusing to let him go. They alleged that his intention to study in Poland wasn't clear enough and that if they released him, he might well stay illegally in Germany. Thiago was outraged at what he was hearing. He knew he had the right to stay there without a visa for three months, so he felt simply violated by these unfounded accusations. But mainly he felt sad and desperate; he was so close, just a couple of hundred kilometers from his goal, and he was going to be sent back to where he'd started. He didn't resist, the policeman beside him looked like a German shepherd on the brink of biting him, and he didn't want to add more injuries to his already offended and injured self. The police gave Thiago's passport to the plane captain and asked him to give it back once they arrived in Sao Paulo. When he got his passport back, not even a stamp had been put on it. It was as if he'd never been to Germany.